RABID

HOLLY S ROBERTS

WICKED STORY TELLING

CONTENTS

THRILLERS BY HOLLY

Morgan Family Thrillers
RABID
LONG PIG
WILLOW (2026)
Carter Family Shark Thrillers
BREACH
CHURN
DEPTH
Shark Thriller
SIXGILL (2026)
Detective Eve Bennet Crime Series
ONLY GIRL ALIVE
LOST LITTLE ANGELS
PRAY FOR HER
Marinah and the Apocalypse Series
SHADOW
WARRIOR
BEAST
QUEEN
PRINCESS

PROLOGUE

THE BITE

Rabies is nearly 100% fatal once symptoms appear, but it is almost entirely preventable with timely treatment. The vaccine for rabies was one of the first developed by Louis Pasteur in 1885, and it remains highly effective. Wildlife vaccination programs, such as those using baited rabies vaccines, have helped control the spread of the disease in wild populations, particularly among bats, raccoons, and coyotes.

People who are bitten by wild animals or animals that could be rabid are advised to receive post-exposure prophylaxis (PEP). Each year, about 60,000 Americans receive PEP after potential exposure to rabies. But what if they don't...

***

The rabbit's small nose twitched as it sniffed the scrub grass, each inhale shaky, broken by a dull ache where the predator's teeth had pierced its flesh. The memory of those sharp fangs haunted him, his tiny body quivering as the seconds replayed in his mind. Somehow, he had escaped. But how? He didn't know. His thoughts fluttered like fragile leaves caught in a storm—disjointed, frantic.

He nibbled at the grass, forcing his mind to focus on food. Shelter would come next, but hunger gnawed at him. There was something wrong, a strange unease crawling just beneath his fur, but it was distant... for now. He chewed slowly, oblivious to the invader already working its way deeper into his veins.

A day passed, and the unease spread. The rabbit knew something was wrong. He was restless, his mind clouded by a strange, buzzing anxiety that tightened around him, smothering his thoughts. Sunlight became too sharp, stabbing at his eyes, and the slightest sound—the rustle of leaves, the whisper of wind—sent him into fits of panic. Every shadow held a threat.

Another day, and the terror bloomed. He was trapped inside himself, overwhelmed by a compulsion to run, to flee, though he didn't know where. The burrow he had dug now felt like a tomb, its walls closing in, heavy with the scent of fear. His muscles twitched uncontrollably, and no amount of scratching could reach the itch deep in his bones. Food no longer mattered. His body was rebelling, and he didn't know why.

Night blurred into day, time losing all meaning. The rabbit lashed out at invisible enemies, biting at the air, his movements jerky and wild. His throat tightened, and he couldn't swallow. Each attempt brought a rising panic. Water, the thing he needed most, became something to fear. His body had turned against him, each nerve on fire, his mind unraveling into chaos.

The end was a storm of terror and confusion. Trapped inside his own skin, his limbs stiffened, and the world dissolved into a haze of pain and fear. He no longer recognized anything—friend, foe, or otherwise. Everything was a threat. Exhaustion weighed down his small frame as his muscles twitched uncontrollably. His eyes, once bright and alert, glazed over, dull and lifeless. He dragged himself from the burrow, collapsing in the open air.

"I'll help you, sweet bunny," a voice broke through the haze. The girl bent down, lifting the rabbit's trembling body with gentle hands.

Then, a sharp gasp. "Ow, you bit me!" She pulled her hand back, watching the blood bead from the tiny wound. "But I forgive you," she whispered.

The rabbit twitched, a final shudder as life slipped away. The virus surged with renewed energy.

Ah, at last... another host.

I slip in unnoticed, a quiet trespasser, creeping through the tiny break in her skin. She doesn't feel me. Just a little prick, nothing to worry about. I spread, fast and quiet, sinking into her veins, riding her blood toward her nerves, inching ever closer to her brain. Soon, I will take control.

She will be mine.

Her body will bend to my will. Her bite will spread my legacy. Fear will follow her, an omen for my power. Her story will end, as they all do, but I will live on.

I am rabies.

I am unstoppable.

Chapter One

The Quiet Danger

JOAN MORGAN PLOWED THE soil gently, using one hand to push the shovel into the dirt and the other to pull potatoes from the ground by the roots. The crop sustained her throughout the summer, and into the winter when snowstorms made the hour-long drive to town impossible. The nights were cool, but the days were already unseasonably hot. Even with the greenhouse shielding her from the June sun, sweat trickled down her face.

She lived on eighty acres in northeastern Arizona, a stretch of high desert known as Juniper Springs Ranch. The name was misleading. There wasn't a spring in sight. The only water came from the largest aquifer in Arizona, hidden beneath thousands of acres of rock-laden, shrub-filled land. The ranch had once belonged to a cattle family, but after the business failed, they sold off parcels. Joan, like most of the locals, called it *the ranch*.

She purchased her land for a literal steal. The previous owner had been sentenced to federal prison for scamming people out of their money. The government auctioned off his property, including a three-thousand-square-foot garage intended to store antique cars. The government sold the cars too, but Joan didn't care. Her old '75 Ford truck was all she needed. The property had a well, septic, and solar power, and at eighty-five grand, the garage that would become her house fit neatly into her cash-only budget. That was fifteen years ago, when she'd been fifty-five and eager for hard work to forget the past.

Now it was her sanctuary, where she could thrive off the grid and find peace most of the time. She had once been a city girl, unfamiliar with self-reliance, but now she had learned to fend for herself. She relished the challenges she faced, even as age crept into her bones and joints.

Max's low growl interrupted her thoughts. She couldn't see him from the greenhouse, but she knew the hundred-and-fifty-pound Rottweiler's growl wasn't his usual one. This was higher-pitched, unsettled. He may have cornered another groundhog. She wiped the sweat from her face with the back of her hand, smearing dirt across her cheek, and tipped back the brim of her oversized gardening hat. The next bark, sharp and strange, sent a chill through her. She set the shovel down, grabbed the shotgun leaning against the greenhouse wall, and headed toward the sound. Whatever had riled Max, it was better to handle it now than let this escalate.

She had to harvest the potatoes before the weather grew too hot. The greenhouse allowed her to plant through the winter, but the potatoes didn't like summer heat. She would be able to harvest the second planter box again before the winter snow hit. Most of her other plants thrived throughout the year and gave her plenty to eat and ample work to keep her busy.

Max's growling gave her an excuse to take a break and grab a glass of water. The gnats outside made it impossible to drink without them swarming her glass, so she had left it on an inside table.

Another bark, more frantic this time. Her pace quickened. When Max had a problem, it was best to figure it out before he decided to take matters into his own paws.

Today's temperature pushed eighty degrees. Mother Nature had thrown in an early heat wave, complete with clouds of dust and swarms of gnats. Joan wiped a gnat from her nose and kept moving. She preferred the heat over the cold, though, and tried not to complain.

She rounded the house but didn't see Max. A sharp yelp from behind the barn sent her in that direction. She heard a whisper before she spotted the dog.

"Shush, you're giving away my hiding spot, you dumb dog."

"Carrie?" Joan called out, concern rising in her voice.

"Go away," came the child's reply, soft and defiant.

"You know you can't be here," Joan scolded gently.

Despite Carrie's contrary behavior, Joan had grown fond of her. Carrie's brothers would come looking for her soon enough, and Joan wanted her gone before they arrived. They were as mean-spirited as their father. Joan glanced toward the road. No sign of them yet. Good.

Max let out another low whine, staying five feet away from Carrie. This was odd behavior for him. He never growled at her, at least not until today. Joan knelt down to take a closer look at him. She swore the dog could read her thoughts; another whine escaped his throat, and his eyes shifted toward Carrie and back to hers. He was protective by nature, a gentle giant, but something had him spooked.

Joan squatted down to see the girl hiding beneath a few two-by-fours leaning against the side of the barn. The wood offered a scrap of shade, just enough to hide her small frame. A reddened face peered out from the shadows.

Carrie was small for her age, with the telltale signs of neglect and malnourishment. Dirt streaked her pale skin, bruises marring her thin arms and legs. Her hair, a brown tangled mess, clung to her forehead, matted and unkempt. The sadness in her eyes was far too deep for a child so young. She rarely smiled, and when she did, it flickered and disappeared almost instantly, as if she'd forgotten how.

"Come out," Joan said softly. "You can have a glass of water and a cookie, but then you need to go home before we both get into trouble."

Carrie had been visiting Joan for four years, ever since the day she'd appeared at the doorstep asking for food. She'd said nothing about her family or her life, only that she was hungry. Joan had given her a bowl of leftover rice, and before she could ask pointed questions, the child had run off. That was the beginning of their strange, unspoken friendship.

The first time, Joan had been so disturbed by the encounter that she called the sheriff's department. Dale Berger, a deputy who lived about five miles from her, came out the next day and took a report. His response hadn't eased her worries.

"No missing children have been reported," he said, tipping his hat back. "A new family moved into the old Tanner homestead. They've got a pack of kids, and they've got attitude. Best to steer clear."

And that was that.

With a sigh over the memory, Joan held out her hand. Carrie moved, but slowly. "I don't feel good," she whispered, rubbing her eyes.

Joan reached into the small space, feeling the girl's forehead. It was warm, but then, so was the day. She'd only checked out of habit. "Come on," she coaxed, helping Carrie to her feet.

Max sniffed the girl again, then backed away, whining once more. Whatever it was, he didn't like it. Considering he rolled in dead animals any chance he got, his aversion was almost comical. Joan smelled nothing unusual. The stench of unwashed clothes and filth that seemed to follow Carrie and her family was normal. They operated an illegal puppy mill, and their home stank of urine and feces. Whether it came from dogs or people, Joan didn't want to know.

She had learned to stop judging unwashed bodies. Many of the homesteaders who bought forty-acre lots in the area lived similarly, minus the puppy mill. Some didn't even have wells, hauling water from town in large containers. Life was hard out here, and Joan had adjusted. She'd come to the ranch for a reason. It took her out of the media frenzy that surrounded her daughter's death. The land offered her isolation and a place to heal.

"Come on," she said, taking Carrie's small hand in hers. "Let's get you inside."

Joan led Carrie into the house, Max trailing behind but keeping his distance. Something about the child had unsettled him, and Joan felt slightly disconcerted. She opened the metal security door and leaned the shotgun against the inside wall. The cool, shadowed interior of the house was a relief after the heat outside.

Joan turned on the ceiling fan, stirring the air. Funny, she thought, how living off-grid had made her conscious of every bit of energy she used. She could remember the days when she'd leave the fan running without a second thought, but her life now felt more deliberate, more... pure. She crossed the room and poured Carrie a glass of filtered water, handing it to her before setting two cookies on a paper towel.

Carrie took a drink, but almost immediately, she began coughing. Her hand flew to her throat, and she set the glass down, a shudder running through her. Joan frowned, watching as Carrie's small hand trembled, her fingers twitching in a way that didn't seem right.

"Does your throat hurt?" Joan asked, her concern deepening.

Carrie nodded, her face flushed. Then, her entire body trembled for about two seconds before it stopped. Joan handed her the cookies, but instead of eating them like she usually did, Carrie slipped them into her pocket.

"Okay," Joan said gently. "I'll give you something for your throat, but you can't tell your father." She hated making a child keep secrets, but Jeb Hogg would raise hell if he found out she'd given Carrie medicine. Carrie nodded again, her movements slow and lethargic.

Joan reached up to the small cabinet where she kept basic medicines; ibuprofen, some cough syrup, nothing major. She didn't like taking pills herself, but she kept a few things on hand for emergencies. She handed Carrie two tablets, but when she offered the glass of water again, Carrie simply chewed them dry, her expression unchanged despite what must have been a bitter taste.

Max growled, low and steady, his eyes fixed on the front door.

A moment later, Joan heard the rumble of a truck engine.

"Carrie, you in there?" a voice called from outside. Joan recognized it immediately. One of Carrie's brothers.

All but Carrie knew better than to come onto Joan's property without permission. The boys would park at the entrance to her drive. Joan might be old, but she had no problem chasing off the Hogg boys with a shotgun in hand. Joan's dislike of the Hogg family was something she struggled with, but she couldn't help it. They were cruel, dangerous people.

Carrie glanced up at Joan, her bloodshot eyes wide and glassy. Slowly, she made her way to the door, pausing only to give Joan one last look before stepping outside.

"Pop's gonna tan your hide," her brother sneered as she approached the truck.

Joan followed her to the door, her hand resting on the shotgun just in case. "She's not feeling well," she called out, her voice steady. "Take her straight to your mother. She needs care."

The boy sneered at Joan and backhanded Carrie across the side of her head. "Shut up," he spat, before kicking at the dirt and glaring at Joan. He turned and climbed into the truck's bed, dragging Carrie along with him.

Joan stood at the door, her grip tightening on the shotgun, watching as the truck kicked up a cloud of dust and disappeared down the road.

She stood there until they were out of sight. Only then did the heavy weight settle in her chest. The years of fighting the Hogg family weren't over, and she was growing weary. Giving up wasn't an option. Willow had to have a safe place.

Joan didn't know it yet, but her world was about to change for the worse. It was the last time she saw Carrie alive.

CHAPTER TWO

HOGG DARN SECRETS

The Past

IT HAD BEEN DAYS since Joan first saw the little girl, and she couldn't get the image out of her mind. A child that young, barefoot, filthy, and alone in the middle of nowhere; it didn't sit right with her. She'd reported it to the sheriff's department, but nothing had come of it. Deputy Berger had brushed off her concerns as if she'd imagined the whole thing.

His attitude hadn't satisfied Joan. No child should be wandering alone in this harsh environment. There were rattlesnakes and mountain lions, and in packs, even coyotes could be a threat. She tried to keep an eye out for the girl after that, but there was no sign of her. Still, the image lingered of the small, frightened, hungry child.

Then there were the sounds. Ever since that strange encounter, Joan had noticed barking and howling coming from the direction of the old Tanner homestead. The noise had an edge to it, almost desperate, like the animals were crying out in pain or fear. It wasn't normal. The howling would start every evening at feeding time and stretch on for an hour, a low, mournful sound that chilled her to the bone.

The unease gnawed at her, mixing with her frustration over Deputy Berger's lack of action. But she had other things to focus on. It was Tuesday, and in three days, she'd see her granddaughter, Willow. That was her comfort. She could feel Willow's arms around her, grounding her, giving a reprieve from the dark and troubling thoughts that plagued her.

Joan glanced at her new puppy, who was dozing in the shade.

"I'll keep you close until I know more about those dogs," she murmured, glancing toward the far-off homestead.

The barking made her uneasy, though the source was still far enough away not to be a direct threat—yet.

When she'd returned from picking up the puppy at the airport, she found her shed broken into and a few tools missing. It didn't take much guessing to figure out who was responsible. The new family at the Tanner place, the Hoggs as she would learn, were trouble, plain and simple. Joan had heard enough from Berger's warning, but seeing the damage and missing items confirmed it for her. She hadn't even bothered calling the sheriff this time. Nothing would be done.

Still, it gnawed at her. She wasn't the type to sit by and do nothing. She believed in helping people, especially children like the little girl she'd seen. In her mind it was atonement for her granddaughter Willow, and she would pay for the remainder of her life. If her neighbors were stealing from her, maybe meeting them face-to-face would set some boundaries. If she introduced herself, she might get a better sense of what was happening out there, and if the girl needed help.

With that thought, she packed up a plate of homemade chocolate chip cookies for the kids and loaded them in her truck, Lucy, for the short drive over. The road was rough, narrow, and lined with scraggly bushes that whipped against the side of the old paint. Lucy grumbled beneath her as the wheels rolled over the ruts and rocks in the dirt road, but the familiar sound calmed Joan's nerves.

The homestead appeared ahead, and Joan's stomach tightened. The house, if you could call it that, was more of a crumbling shack with patches of tarps and rusted metal sheets thrown together to cover holes. Old vehicle tires rested on the roof to keep it from blowing away. Dog kennels, poorly constructed, were scattered across the yard, their chain-link doors barely held together. The barking had only grown louder as she approached, a cacophony of yelps and cries from the dozens of dogs crammed into the tiny spaces.

Her heart sank. This was worse than she'd imagined.

A man appeared from around the side of the barn, a shotgun slung over his shoulder. He was short and stocky, with grimy jeans and an oil-stained shirt. His eyes narrowed against the sun. His hair was long and greasy, his face scruffy and unshaven. He stopped in his tracks, anger radiating off him in waves.

"What do you want?" he called, his voice rough as gravel. A large brindle-colored dog stood by his side.

Joan studied the canine. He was a muscular, compact force of nature, all sinewy strength beneath a coat of multi-colored stripes that gave it a wild, feral look. Its wide, powerful chest led to a thick neck that seemed to bunch with tension, as if barely holding back its aggression. Sharp amber eyes glared out from beneath a low brow, alert and distrustful, completely predatory, almost daring her to challenge. Scars peppered its face and shoulders, tokens of countless fights, each one etched into its short, bristling fur. Its lips pulled back in a low, menacing snarl, exposing slightly yellowed teeth that gleamed with a promise of violence.

Joan stepped away from the truck, balancing the plate of cookies in her hand, forcing a smile she didn't feel.

"I'm your neighbor, Joan Morgan. I live down the road." She held the plate out slightly. "Thought I'd come by, introduce myself, and bring cookies for the kids."

The man's eyes flicked to the plate, then back to her face. He didn't move. From behind him, a woman emerged, thin and gaunt, her dress hanging loosely from her small frame. Her head was down, and she barely glanced at Joan before retreating toward the house. A small figure clung to her skirt. It was the hungry little girl. Her wide eyes locked onto Joan's for a moment, and she shook her head sharply before she, too, disappeared behind the woman.

"You want to please my kids, huh?" the man sneered, his voice dripping with sarcasm. "Well, we don't need nothin' from you."

Joan's forced smile faltered.

"I just wanted to say hello. You know, in case you ever need anything."

He took a step forward, his eyes narrowing as he adjusted the shotgun on his shoulder. The brindle's low growl gained force with its owner's tone.

"We won't ever need your help. And your damn cookies can go in the trash for all I care."

The boys appeared. Four of them, the youngest about fourteen, each with the same hostile glare. Dirt and grime seemed embedded into their very being. They didn't say anything, just stood there, arms crossed, watching her like a pack of wolves waiting for the signal to attack.

Joan swallowed, her grip tightening on the plate. This was a mistake. She should have stayed home. She hadn't realized the depth of the hostility here, the danger lurking just beneath the surface. Deputy Berger had tried to warn her.

"Well," she said, her voice quiet but steady, "if you change your mind, you know where to find me."

The man grunted, his face twisting into a sneer as he jerked his head toward the driveway.

"Get off my land."

Joan didn't argue. She turned and climbed back into Lucy, setting the plate on the passenger seat. She started the truck and backed out slowly, keeping her eyes straight ahead. She could feel their gazes burning into her as she drove away.

In the rearview mirror, the crumbling homestead disappeared behind a cloud of dust. She didn't need to see it to know the kind of people living there. Trouble.

As soon as she was out of sight, Joan let out a breath she didn't realize she'd been holding. Her hands shook slightly in anger as she gripped the wheel.

"I'm a damn fool," she muttered to herself. "I should've known better."

She would later learn she'd trespassed on the Hogg family's homestead and Jeb Hogg was the leader of the pack.

CHAPTER THREE

PSYCHOTIC PEACE

Past

J OAN LIVED IN PEACE for years before the Hoggs became her neighbors. Their arrival turned her solitary life into hell. The multiple thefts from her property took away her sense of security, but it was the incessant barking and howling that drove her mad. She had called the sheriff's department numerous times, and nothing changed. After exhausting all other options, she finally resorted to contacting the closest city's humane society. She told them about the puppy mill and the dog fighting.

At night on the ranch, you could see car lights coming for miles. There was never a pattern where she could pinpoint the next fight, but she knew at least ten different vehicles, with an unknown number of passengers, attended them. The horrible sounds on those nights were indescribable.

The person she spoke with was sympathetic. They'd also said that without a police report, evidence was needed for them to get involved. Joan pondered the problem and came up with a solution. She couldn't pinpoint the fights, but she could almost certainly capture animal abuse in the lens of her camera.

On a particularly warm evening a week later, Joan decided to collect the evidence. It could take several trips, and she didn't care. Listening to the sounds of tortured dogs was at an end. She left Max behind so she could sneak in and out quickly.

Over the years, Joan had hiked every inch of her property, and by following the wash through the canyon and navigating the ridge, she would come out above the Hoggs' homestead. It was the perfect spot to spy, and she held no illusions. This was spying.

She'd waited for the full moon so she wouldn't need a flashlight, though she brought a small one. She also had binoculars and a good camera.

"You behave while I'm gone and don't chew the furniture," Joan told Max and handed him a bully bone that would hopefully keep him busy. He was a year old now, but she'd found him gnawing on one of her old shoes a few days before, and they were her favorite gardening pair.

He looked at her with the same sad eyes he always had when she left him behind. He opened his jaws and made a small noise; that was his way of speaking.

"I know," she patted his head. "I'll be back soon. Guard the house."

Joan loved the Rottweiler breed because they inherently knew how to guard their family, and they looked fierce. She'd turned Max into a big baby, but she had no doubt he would protect her at risk to his own life. Rottweilers were basically lazy dogs who liked cool weather over warm and could be stubborn when it came to things like baths. Max was her fourth, and she hadn't thought she would get another after her Molly died, but with mountain lion sightings, she'd needed another dog. He'd helped deter the Hoggs from their petty theft and vandalism too. She felt more secure with him inside at night. He would be okay for a couple of hours no matter what his sorrowful eyes begged for.

Joan stepped from the back door into the muggy night air. Monsoons would start soon and give relief in the afternoons. Most people thought of Arizona as desert, but that was only the southern part of the state. She lived six thousand feet above sea level, and although it was considered high desert, she was able to enjoy all four seasons each year. She prepared for winter at the end of summer and shopped for food storage at the large shopping club store in Flagstaff, which was a little more than two hours away. Flagstaff had one of the highest snowfall accumulations in the country, and winter stopped all but necessary travel. It was something she planned for each year.

Joan turned on the flashlight so she didn't stumble as she hiked down the first ridge to the scrub-filled area before she got to the wash. She carefully made her way down to what she called the flatlands. It was an area about the size of two football fields. She'd thought about planting wildflower seeds just to see what happened. Maybe next spring, she mumbled under her breath as she went around a group of large boulders taller than her.

Dead shaggy-bark junipers and cedar trees littered the area. It was great for collecting kindling. She went up another small ridge to where she could see the wash. It was easier to slide down on her backside than to risk falling, and that's exactly what she did. She couldn't help thinking about the woman who moved out here and the healing it gave her damaged psyche. That weak person was long gone. In her place stood a self-sufficient, capable woman who would figure out a way to do just about anything. The land would give her granddaughter these same traits, and Willow had something else going for her. She was a survivor, and she would fit into this lifestyle just fine, at least if the Hoggs weren't in the picture.

Joan made it to the wash and had to climb down an embankment to the sand. It tired her legs, but the wash was basically clear, and she could avoid large boulders and fallen trees. If she saw water, she sought high ground immediately. Heavy rain in New Mexico sent water cascading into her wash while there were clear skies above her house, and it all started with the first trickle. Joan couldn't help feeling proud of the survival accomplishments she'd made. There wasn't much of a city woman left.

If she'd driven to the Hogg homestead, it would have been a much shorter distance. The problem was Jeb and his sons could see and hear her coming. All she wanted to do was sneak close enough to gather evidence for the sheriff's department and humane society.

She half-crawled up the final ridge, the sandy hill making it hard to find purchase without sliding backward. At the top, she looked around and saw an area of scrub brush with a large bush beside it that would be perfect for surveillance. She couldn't turn on her flashlight and had no idea what critters were on the ground as she bent low and wiggled her body into position, dragging her backpack behind her. This was something else she'd never thought she could do and another accomplishment. She no longer gave a fig about bugs.

Reaching inside the worn leather, she retrieved her camera. It was an older model but had a good fast lens for nighttime photography. She loved taking pictures of her land and the amazing number of stars, along with incredible full moons. Her favorite cactus plant let loose with stunning pinkish-red blossoms for one week each year, adding to her image collection. The camera had become a friend.

A male voice called out, and Joan stopped attaching the lens so she could listen.

"This dog is gonna learn what it's job is or he's going in the fire," Jeb yelled.

Joan finished attaching the lens and pointed the camera at the house. A burning fire pit sat about ten feet away from the front door of the home. Movement to the right had her veering her lens in that direction. One of the Hogg boys held the leash of a medium sized Pitbull. It barked and growled incessantly at another dog cowering behind one of the other boys. Jeb's sons released them at the same time and the Pitbull sprang forward.

Joan watched in horror, a sick feeling rising in her stomach. The fight didn't last long and when it was over, the smaller dog, which no longer moved, was tossed on the fire.

Jeb Hogg was a revolting human being, and his sons weren't far down the list.

Joan moved the lens after getting her trembling hands under control and began capturing Hogg horror.

Kennel after kennel contained multiple dogs. She could only imagine their suffering because most were lying still within the small boxes. She could just make out one with its head between a break in its bars, panting, its muzzle low. She couldn't begin to count the number of dogs.

Anger overwhelmed Joan, and she itched for her shotgun.

If the sheriff's department didn't do something with her evidence, Joan would take the law into her own hands, and the law could arrest her for being a psychotic killer. She took her final pictures and left.

Early the following morning, her anger still in overdrive, she'd driven to Deputy Berger's place. She'd gotten lost twice because she only knew the general vicinity. She finally made the last correct turn and saw the top lights on his police SUV.

He'd listened and taken her evidence, which she'd transferred to a CD.

"This may not be enough," he said.

Joan saw red. "You had better make sure it's enough, or you'll be investigating five homicides."

"Don't be saying that, Joan," he insisted.

"It's Mrs. Morgan to you. For once, do your job. That family is a menace. They treat that girl like their personal punching bag, and I'm tired of your department doing nothing."

The deputy turned and muttered under his breath.

"I can hear you, you old goat. I meant what I said."

She stormed back to her truck and kicked up dust as she slammed it into gear and took off.

Deputy Berger did his job and filed charges. Joan also sent the images to the Humane Society. Unfortunately, they had their own way of doing things and she hadn't understood when she first spoke to them. The judge agreed with their solution. If Jeb turned over his dogs and swore to never own more, his charges would go away, and even his penalty for making the dogs square off would disappear. The judge added insult to injury by saying a video recording of the dog fight might have swayed him.

Joan's testimony meant nothing. What she witnessed and captured in images was worthless.

Jeb took the deal. His new puppy mill was back in full swing within six months. A few months after that, his pit-fighting dogs were heard again too.

The memory of what she'd witnessed didn't leave her and she constantly stewed on the trial's outcome. Joan's extreme dislike of the Hoggs grew to something more.

CHAPTER FOUR

FATE BE DAMNED

Past

JOAN'S DAYS ON HER land were filled with everything from gardening to maintenance in the summer to chopping wood and kindling for winter. Training Max was an ongoing job and one that she loved.

By six months old, his personality was in full bloom. He was the smartest of her Rottweilers, and she didn't think it possible. He wanted nothing more than to please her. Well, cookies. He wanted those too.

He trailed behind her everywhere. She taught him to carry items. She trained him to help pull. His desire to learn was endless, and she knew if she were hurt somewhere out on her property, Max would get her home.

Joan had rescued her first Rottweiler when the secretary who worked beside her at the phone company went through a divorce. She couldn't take the dog, Ruffus, out of state with her. Joan was lonely. Her daughter Sammy had left years before, and Joan needed companionship that had nothing to do with men.

She'd never considered herself a dog person, but Ruffus changed that. The way he communicated with expressions, whines, and barks lightened her world. Joan became a Rottweiler mom, and it suited her just fine.

When Ruffus died, it broke her heart. Six months later, she'd purchased a five-month-old Rottweiler puppy using part of her precious savings. Within a few weeks, she wondered if she'd made a mistake. The puppy was no Ruffus, and he might eat her house. A friend suggested training, so Joan signed up for a class.

The trainer made it clear on the first day that it was not her job to train the dogs, it was her job to train the owners. Joan learned just how ignorant she was when it came to dog behavior. Ruffus had been moderately trained, didn't pee in the house, and never ate the furniture. Saydee, as a puppy, had none of those qualities.

Joan learned about dog behavior, and another world opened for her. The trainer was so impressed with Joan's willingness to learn that she recommended Joan take the advanced course too.

Saydee, lovingly placed in her new kennel each day when Joan went to work, changed her rotten ways, and their friendship became cemented.

When Saydee's life came to a sudden end after bone cancer was discovered when she was eight, Joan waited only a month to find a new puppy. Her heavy heart barely made it the month. Molly came into her life, and this time, Joan did the training herself and took it to the next level. It was a great hobby, and with work, it gave her little time to worry about her daughter.

Her third dog died a natural death. Things had changed in Joan's life, and she decided: no more dogs.

That lasted through her daughter's death and her granddaughter's murder trial. Joan thought about those years as little as possible and was just happy to live in peace on the ranch, learning how to take care of herself.

Independence suited her, and she was thankful for the phone company stock she'd invested in through the years. It made it possible for Joan to buy the property and survive until her Social Security came through.

Then came Jeb Hogg. The trial gave Jeb a bigger reason to hate her. That was okay because she fully returned the sentiment now. Carrie was the only reason Joan hadn't lit the Hogg house on fire. Okay, that wasn't true. She only wished the place would burn down when they weren't home, and they moved away.

Max was now a necessity more for Hogg deterrence than mountain lions. Jeb's sons loved to speed past her drive, kicking up dust, yelling profanities, and every threat they could think of. They had three brain cells between the four boys, so she tried to ignore the harassment.

"If people didn't live past my road, I would spike it," she told Max after the semiweekly drive-by.

The low rumble that came from his throat made her feel better. He disliked the Hoggs as much as she did. Carrie was another story. Max loved her and thought of her as his extra-special human who gave good belly rubs. It took Carrie a bit to warm up to him due to her father's dogs, but once the trust was established, she gave him as many belly rubs as time allowed.

Carrie's growing comfort with Max mirrored the slow trust building between her and Joan. At first, the girl would barely speak, slipping in and out of the house like a shadow. But over time, Carrie began to linger, eating her meals more slowly, or sitting by the fireplace as Joan worked on a project. Joan had come to love these moments of quiet companionship, where words weren't necessary.

The bond deepened further when Carrie began asking questions. Sometimes they were about the land or the animals, but once in a while, they were personal. Those moments felt precious, like cracks in a wall Carrie had built around herself. Joan had come to care for the girl deeply, and she hated the life Carrie was forced to endure.

She showed up one day with three punctures in her forearm. They were swollen and unnaturally red.

"What happened?" Joan questioned gently.

She always spoke softly and tried not to ask too many questions, or the girl would run away. Carrie was a wild child and had somehow adapted to the unforgiving environment, but Joan now knew that the real danger was Carrie's father.

The small shoulders shrugged, and Carrie didn't answer.

Joan knew a dog bite when she saw one.

"Did you show your mom?" Joan asked.

"She's sick."

Joan had learned that was code for "too beat up to take care of her daughter." Joan loved her home; she just had trouble accepting the lifestyle of many of her neighbors. She had a family a few miles in the opposite direction from the Hoggs who escaped a religious cult. There were several wives attached to one man, with an unknown number of children. The county didn't monitor which kids went to school and which didn't. Most of the children on the ranch were so-called home-schooled. It meant the kids could learn to feed, water, and fetch firewood, but couldn't add more than two digits.

There she went again, with her judgment. She shook the negative thoughts off, angry at herself for placing blame when she only knew part of the story. The plural wives she'd met were closed off, though never unfriendly, and their children were the same.

With a sigh, Joan examined Carrie's wounds carefully. The young girl didn't even grimace when Joan cleaned them and placed antibiotic ointment over the shallow punctures.

"Want a sandwich?" Joan asked.

Carrie nodded and followed her to the kitchen, Max her steady companion. When her granddaughter Willow came home, Max would love her too.

Joan did most of the talking while Carrie shoveled the food down.

"I have peanut butter today," Joan said when Carrie finished eating.

When she discovered Carrie's love for cookies, only superseded by Max's love for his dog biscuits, she baked a small batch regularly, so she always had them on hand.

She held the cookie back when Carrie placed her hand out.

"Was it the brindle?" she asked, her eyes tipping to the bite.

A stubborn gleam entered Carrie's eyes while her sharp gaze remained on the cookie. Finally, she nodded.

Sweets made great bribes.

Jeb treated his wife and daughter abominably. He loved that brindle, though. That dog was mean and vicious, and the world would be a better place if it were put down. Jeb enjoyed using the dog to terrify Carrie. This wasn't the first bite. The last one, a few months before, had been on the back of her calf. Jeb had sent the dog out to find Carrie, and the bite had been the result.

Deputy Berger tried to explain that they only had two deputies for hundreds of miles and their court system was backed up. It was well known that most of the families were avoiding government control. The county was the perfect fit for people like Jeb Hogg.

"Do you want to read one of your books?" Joan asked her after the cookie was gobbled down in a few bites. Joan had ordered several books she thought Carrie would enjoy.

Carrie shook her head and left through the back door. She would sneak back onto the Hogg property and most likely still be in trouble. She was one tough child, and that in itself was the saddest part.

Joan's dislike of Jeb Hogg had grown to anger, and now that anger simmered just below the boiling point.

CHAPTER FIVE

FATHER HOGG

PRESENT

Jeb Hogg tossed the thin strip of meat onto the makeshift grill, little more than a circle of rocks with a rusted grate propped up by sticks. He yanked off his grimy ball cap and swatted at the smoke with it, his irritation building by the second. His wife, useless as ever, was too broken to cook, and that damn girl had run off again. Let her starve, he thought, wiping sweat from his forehead with the back of his grimy hand. If she'd gone to the old woman's place, there'd be hell to pay when she got back.

The meat sizzled, and his mouth watered. His favorite fighter approached the grill, sniffing at the air, drawn to the scent of blood.

"You touch that, and you'll be humping the ladies on three legs," Jeb growled, tossing the cap at the dog.

The brindle, a Boxer-Pitbull mix Jeb had bred and raised for fighting, bared his teeth but backed off. Jeb grabbed a rock from the ground and hurled it. The dog bolted, skittering across the dirt yard before disappearing under the rusted hulk of an old pickup, his orange eyes glowing from the shadows, a low growl rumbling in his chest.

With ninety-five pounds of muscle and a bad attitude, the dog was king of the pack. He'd earned that title in blood, fighting for dominance whenever provoked. The others knew better than to challenge him, and that included Jeb's four sons. One of them, after a run-in with the brindle, now bore scars along his calf, a lesson learned the hard way. Jeb had laughed it off, told the boy to clean the wound, and get back to work.

"What about that worthless mutt?" one of his sons hollered from the porch.

"He's the best damn fighter and breeder I've got. His balls are twice the size of yours. Get closer, and he'll make sure you've got none left." His son stormed back into the house, slamming the door behind him.

Jeb smirked, tearing off a bite of the nearly raw meat, juice and blood smearing his lips when he popped it into his mouth. The burn from the hot flesh set his nerves on fire, and he cursed, chewing angrily. His temper, already hanging by a thread, flared up, feeding off the pain. He looked up as his truck roared up the dirt road, kicking up a thick cloud of dust. His daughter sat in the bed of the truck, and his fury deepened. He stayed where he was, savoring the moment. There was something about watching the girl walk toward him, knowing what was coming.

Carrie jumped from the truck and darted toward the house, her head low, avoiding his gaze. He was on his feet in seconds.

"Get your ass over here," Jeb bellowed.

She froze. Slowly, she turned, her steps dragging as though every inch was a battle. Her skin was pale, almost gray, and sweat streaked her dirt-smeared face. Her movements were jerky, her thin arms trembling as she struggled to keep herself upright. Jeb saw none of it. All he saw was disobedience.

When he couldn't stand her hesitation any longer, he closed the distance, his hand shooting out to backhand her, knuckles cracking against her cheek. She crumpled to the ground in silence, curling into a ball as he towered over her, seething. Grabbing her with a huge handful of hair, he yanked her to her feet, forcing her to look at him.

"You went to that old bitch's house, didn't you?" His voice was low and venomous, hot breath against her face. "You worthless piece of shit."

Carrie's wide, reddened eyes stared up at him. Her fever-bright gaze flickered, a wild glaze creeping over her features as her limbs jerked uncontrollably. Jeb didn't notice. He saw only defiance, or what he took for it. His hand tightened in her hair, shaking her roughly. His anger boiled over, but before he could strike again, pain shot through his arm. Carrie's teeth had sunk into his wrist, clamped down hard enough to draw blood.

Jeb roared, releasing her and pounding his fist against her head until she let go, her jaws slackening. He stared at the puncture marks, red beads welling up from where her teeth had broken the skin. His boot lashed out, catching her square in the ribs. He didn't stop until she was limp and silent.

Only then did his sons drag him away, muttering about how "Da's gone off again." But even they paused when they noticed the unnatural way Carrie's body twitched, her shallow breaths rattling in her chest.

"Get that worthless piece of trash out of my sight," Jeb spat, turning back to the grill to tear off another strip of meat, still muttering curses under his breath. He glanced down at the bloody bite on his arm, a grim smile curling his lips as he headed toward the barn to check on his latest litter.

Carrie never regained consciousness.

Chapter Six

Simmering Anger

ONCE A MONTH, JOAN drove four hours to see her grand-daughter, Willow, and it never got easier. But this time, her thoughts were scattered. Carrie's gaunt face kept flashing in her mind, the tremor in her hands, the fever in her eyes. Something was wrong with that child, and it gnawed at Joan even before she left home.

Max whined from the doorway as if sensing her unease. He pawed at the floor, restless.

"I know," Joan said softly, bending down to scratch behind his ears. "I'll be back tonight, and you'll be just fine. I can't trust Jeb not to come around, so you're staying inside."

Big brown eyes stared at her, his ears pinned back, giving her the saddest look imaginable. He understood. He always had. Besides her favorite garden shoes when he was a puppy, he'd never chewed on another item of hers. She gave him one last empathetic look and locked the heavy security door, ensuring her house was safe before heading to the truck.

Lucy, her old Ford, had been with her for decades. It sputtered as she turned the key but roared to life after a couple of grumbles. Eva Cassidy's soft, haunting voice filled the cab after Joan slid a cassette into the player. The music soothed her nerves as she headed out, the wide, barren desert landscape unfolding around her.

She tried to focus on the road ahead, but her mind kept circling back to Carrie. The child's flushed face had seemed even more fragile than usual. She was always too thin, too quiet, but this time was different. The jerky movements, the fever. It was strange. Things like hantavirus were a very real possibility, especially with their homestead likely mouse- and rat-infested.

Joan tightened her grip on the steering wheel. She had done what she could, but it never felt like enough. The thought of leaving Carrie behind made her stomach twist. For a fleeting moment, she considered turning around, going back to check on her. But what would she do? Jeb would never let her help, and calling the sheriff felt useless. Still, the doubt lingered.

As she drove, her thoughts shifted to Willow. Her granddaughter was trapped in that horrible place, locked behind concrete walls and steel bars. Joan tried not to dwell on the past, but the memories were always there, haunting the edges of her thoughts, especially during these long drives.

Joan's husband, Larry, died when Sammy was four years old. Joan thought she loved him when they married, but it was soon apparent he was not the man he pretended to be. He didn't want her to work or attend college, which had been her dream. He'd outright refused and demanded she stay home. They barely had enough to get by, and she became good at juggling the monthly bills.

After Larry's death in a freak accident, she'd needed money. There were few full-time jobs available for women in the fifties, and secretary work was all she could find. It did, however, pay the bills, and she didn't spend money at the bar each night like he had, so she found herself slightly better off financially, and far better mentally.

Sammy, as a teenager, had been wild and rebellious. Their fights had often ended in shouting matches that left them both exhausted. Joan had held firm on curfew and a few rules, but it had never been enough to keep Sammy from repeatedly testing every limit.

Her daughter met Todd and introduced him to Joan only once. A week later, they took off in the middle of the night, leaving only a foul-worded note behind. It broke Joan's heart, but Sammy was now eighteen, and there was nothing she could do. The consequences of Sammy's actions would eventually kill her.

The justice system had twisted the story of Sammy and Todd's violent deaths, and the media had mangled it even further. But it was Joan's guilt that haunted her the most. What if she had done something differently? What if she had been softer in some places and harder in others? Would Sammy still be alive? Those same questions pushed her to keep trying for Willow, to be someone who wouldn't give up.

There was no going back, no changing the past. But Joan still carried the weight of those unanswered questions. She often wondered how much Sammy had suffered. Joan knew Willow continued to endure horrible circumstances. She had seen it in her granddaughter's eyes during every visit: the guilt, the sadness, and the fierce strength it had taken to survive.

The miles stretched on, the barren road leading her into the tall trees of the mountains, and next into the lower desert. At a small gas station about an hour and a half from her destination, Joan stopped to use the restroom. She grabbed a pack of breath mints at the counter, feeling a slight pang of guilt for not bringing anything to Willow. But they didn't allow visitors to bring gifts. The only time she could send anything was on holidays and birthdays, and even then, the process was filled with rigid rules.

She climbed back into Lucy, starting the final leg of the journey. The prison loomed in the distance, rising out of the landscape like a menacing monument, barbed wire curling along the tops of the fences like a crown of thorns. Joan's stomach twisted in knots. She hated seeing Willow in this place. Hated knowing her granddaughter was locked away, treated like a criminal when she had only done what she'd had to do to stay alive.

Joan pulled into the parking lot; her heart heavy as she stepped out of the truck. The sun beat down, but the air was much hotter here, as if the weight of the sun sucked all enjoyment from the world.

She approached the entrance gate, pressing the button for the intercom.

"I'm Joan Morgan, here to visit Willow Humphrey," she said, her tone steady despite the tightness in her chest.

The disembodied voice on the other end rattled off the usual instructions: what she could and couldn't bring inside, the penalties for breaking the rules. Joan had heard it all before, so many times that the words had become background noise.

The buzzer sounded, and Joan pushed the door open, stepping inside. The sterile smell of the lobby hit her immediately, and she approached the desk to hand over her driver's license. The guard behind the counter was new, she didn't recognize him. It didn't matter. They all rotated out eventually, and Joan had long since stopped keeping track of the faces.

"I'll buzz you through once the inmate is ready," the guard said, his tone flat.

Joan nodded and moved to the side, waiting in the sparse lobby. There were no chairs, no comforts. This place wasn't designed for visitors to feel welcome. She shifted on her feet, glancing at the clock as the minutes ticked by.

Soon, she would see Willow. She would wrap her arms around her granddaughter and feel that fleeting moment of connection, the warmth of family that was so rare in this place. Joan couldn't stop the thoughts racing through her mind. Carrie's condition, Sammy's fate, and Willow's resilience. It all tangled together in the stillness.

For now, all she could do was wait. She had already waited so many years, but worse, so had Willow.

Chapter Seven

Jeb Hogg Hell

S EVERAL DAYS HAD PASSED since his worthless daughter had put up her last fight. Jeb woke up this morning with an odd tingling sensation on his arm where the bitch had bitten him. His throat felt dry, and when he drank water from the jug, it felt uncomfortable to swallow. It didn't help that his head ached, and he was tired. He had a big money fight coming up and it would be a long day working with the dogs. He didn't have time for this shit.

"Boys, where the hell are you?" he yelled as soon as he left the bedroom.

The youngest stuck his head around the corner. "We're here, Da. We already fed and watered the dogs. Ma has breakfast made."

He turned the corner, and his wife, her face tear-streaked, didn't look up. It irritated the shit out of him, and he walked over and smacked her on the back of the head. "What's your problem?" he growled.

"Nothing," she muttered and wiped her cheeks. "I made your favorite."

"And it most likely tastes like shit because all your food tastes like shit."

She visibly trembled, and that pissed him off more. His arm swung out, and he caught her on the jaw. She went to her knees, completely overreacting, and covered her face and cried.

"Get the hell out of here," he yelled. "I want to enjoy my meal even if it's dog slop."

She ran, and that gave him something to smile about. If she wasn't careful, she would end up like Carrie.

The boys stayed quiet through the confrontation, and for some reason, even that irritated him. "What you starin' at?" he demanded.

"Nothin', Da," they said in unison.

"Nothin', my ass," he grumbled. One of the boys dropped his cup on the floor, and the sound rang through Jeb's head, digging the headache in deeper. He ate the slop and left his plate and cup behind.

When he walked outside, the sunlight seemed too bright. He squinted to avoid it and blamed it on the headache. The brindle met him at the door. Jeb didn't bend to pet him as he usually would. He went outside and took a piss over the side of the porch.

The dogs started barking when he approached the barn, and the sound was too loud. It increased his agitation even more. He opened the barn and had to step back at the smell. If he didn't feel better after an hour's work, he would go to bed, and his sons could handle the rest of the day. They weren't good for much, but he was most likely coming down with something, and they could make do.

He fed his dogs just enough to keep them in fighting shape and, at the same time, keep them hungry. A few hours before a fight, he gave them gunpowder wrapped in a piece of meat to make them meaner. When they won, they got a good meal. Sometimes, they weren't hungry after eating part of the dog they killed. The dogs were very aware that Jeb didn't like to lose.

He kicked a couple of the lower cages, deciding which dog he would bring out first. He chose one to start the morning's training and pulled him out, slip-knotted the leash, and put it over his head.

"Grab one of the bait dogs," he told his sons, "and let's see if this one lasts a few rounds."

When he stepped from the barn, the light attacked his eyes again. He felt someone watching him, spying and minding his business. He gazed around the property without noticing anything unusual. His irritation spiked higher.

"It's probably that old bitch," he muttered under his breath. The woman had been a thorn in his side since he moved here. She was one of those do-gooders, and she was the reason his daughter deserved what she got. If the old woman wouldn't have meddled, he wouldn't have had to beat Carrie. He thought about the bite on his arm. No way did she grow a backbone without help, and he knew exactly who helped her.

As the day dragged on, beads of sweat covered his skin, and he felt chilled. He made it a few hours before he went inside and fell into bed fully clothed. He had no idea how long he slept when the nightmare started. A surreal image of Carrie flashed in and out. The dogs attacked her and took her to the ground. He cheered them on until they were covered in blood, and Carrie's body was gone. His eyes popped open. There was movement in the corner of his room. He sprang from the bed and grabbed his shotgun, firing it at the shadow.

Nothing was there. His head ached for real now. No one in his worthless family came to check on him. He drank more water, but it didn't go down right, and he threw the jug against the wall. The noise of the plastic hurt his eardrums, and he swore.

Where the fuck was his family? He fell back into bed. On the edge of sleep, a sense of dread crept in, and his eyes opened. The old bitch stood over him, her expression haunting.

"I'm going to kill you," he whispered before closing his eyes.

CHAPTER EIGHT

UNWAVERING RAGE

A GUARD PHYSICALLY SEARCHED Joan on the outside of her clothing and ran a metal detector over her before leading her down the long, institutionalized hallway. It stretched endlessly, its sterile walls painted in the kind of pale gray that seemed chosen specifically to suppress hope. Harsh fluorescent lights buzzed overhead, casting sharp, unflattering shadows across the scuffed linoleum floor. Identical steel doors lined each side, their small, reinforced windows hinting at the void beyond. The air was thick with the faint metallic tang of rust and something faintly medicinal, mingling with the underlying staleness of too many lives crammed into too small a space.

The echo of distant footsteps, the hum of the overhead lights, and the distant clang of a shutting door created a strange rhythm, almost like the hallway itself was alive, breathing in a slow, relentless cadence. Signs on the walls: "No Loitering," "Stay Behind the Yellow Line" seemed more like commands than helpful guidelines, the institutionalized language of control.

There was an eerie, crushing monotony to the space, a visual representation of the routine and rules imposed on every person who walked through it. The endless stretch of identical doors and walls created a disorienting sense of sameness, stripping away any individuality.

The atmosphere carried a peculiar chill, not from the temperature but from the absence of humanity. It was as if the hallway had absorbed years of hopelessness, anger, and regret, storing them in its unyielding concrete and steel. For those who walked its length daily, it symbolized both confinement and routine, an inescapable reminder of the system's power.

The prison hallway wasn't just a physical space; it was a psychological one. It pressed down on the mind as much as it directed the body, leaving an indelible mark on everyone who passed through it.

The final door opened, and Willow waited inside. Wrapping her in a tight hug was one of the best parts of Joan's visits. For a moment, the pain, frustration, and worry faded away, replaced by the warmth of her granddaughter's embrace. Joan held her close. Willow's arms were thin but strong, a testament to how she had learned to survive in this harsh environment.

When Joan pulled back, she took a long look at her granddaughter. Willow's eyes, though tired, still held a faint flicker of the bright, curious girl Joan remembered at fifteen. The prison hadn't completely taken that away, not yet.

"I missed you so much," Joan said, her voice soft as she searched Willow's face for signs of how she was really doing.

"I missed you too, Grandma," Willow replied, offering a small smile that didn't quite reach her eyes. "I'm glad you came."

Willow had been in prison since she was fifteen, and it had hardened her in ways Joan hadn't expected. At twenty-three, she still had two more years before she could finally walk free, and Joan clung to the hope that Willow, who never really got to be a child, could have a happy life after release.

They sat together at the small, sterile table in the corner of the visitation room. Joan made sure to sit close enough to touch Willow's arm, offering comfort through the connection.

"I was worried they'd lock you down again," Joan said, trying to keep the tone light but unable to hide the real concern behind her words.

Willow shrugged, her smile fading. "I'm fine. Staying out of trouble." But there was something about the way she said it, something unsaid in her voice that told Joan trouble was never far away in a place like this.

"How's Max?" Willow asked, quickly shifting the topic to safer ground.

Joan chuckled softly. "He's still big and bossy, always acting like he runs the place. He's probably pacing the house right now, wondering when I'll be back to let him out."

Willow smiled again, and this time it touched her eyes. "I can't wait to meet him."

For a long time, they hadn't talked about Willow's release. The idea had seemed too distant, too fragile to hope for. Now it was close, just twenty-three months away. Joan had started to believe Willow might actually make it out and that she'd come home, and they could rebuild their lives together. Sadly, each time they talked, Joan noticed the darkness that chipped away at Willow's soul.

"How are your classes going?" Joan asked, eager to talk about something that could bring a spark of hope into their conversation.

Willow's expression brightened slightly. "Good. Struggling with math, but I've got someone helping me. The other classes are fine."

"That's good," Joan said, feeling a small surge of pride. "I always hated math too. But you're smart. You'll figure it out."

Willow nodded, but her focus seemed to drift, as if her thoughts were already elsewhere. Joan wanted to ask more, to dig deeper into what her granddaughter was really feeling, but she knew pushing too hard might close Willow off. There was only so much they could talk about in the brief time they had together, and Joan didn't want to waste it on difficult topics.

"How's that family next door?" Willow asked, glancing at Joan from the corner of her eye.

The question hit harder than Joan expected. She had told Willow all about the Hoggs, their horrible treatment of Carrie, and how they had made life on the ranch more difficult than it needed to be. Joan's heart ached to think about Carrie, how sick she had seemed the last time she saw her. She hadn't told Willow the latest details yet.

"They're as bad as ever," Joan admitted with a sigh. "Jeb Hogg's still up to no good, and his boys are just as rotten as he is. Carrie's not doing well, though. Something made her sick, and I'm worried about her."

Willow's face tightened with a frown, but she didn't say anything for a moment. "Maybe one day she'll be able to fight back," she said quietly, though there wasn't much conviction in her voice.

"I hope so," Joan replied, feeling the weight of helplessness settle over her. "That child deserves better."

Their time together always flew by too fast. Even though Joan cherished every moment, she couldn't shake the dread of knowing their visit was ticking down to the end. She reached over and squeezed Willow's hand. "You'll be home soon," she said, though her voice cracked slightly.

Willow nodded, but the look in her eyes was distant, as if she couldn't quite believe it herself.

Joan hugged her again, feeling the comfort of her arms, hating that this was all they had. She pressed a kiss on Willow's cheek and then forced herself to pull away. Leaving was the hardest part, but if she lingered, she would break down, and she couldn't let Willow see that. Not here.

As Joan made her way out of the prison, the weight of the place seemed to cling to her, adding trepidation to each step she took. The drive back home felt longer, heavier with each mile. She thought about the Hoggs again, about Carrie. Joan knew something terrible was going to happen, she just didn't know what or when.

When she finally turned the last corner toward her house, her heart leapt into her throat. A figure stood there, shining a flashlight directly at her truck.

Her pulse quickened. What the heck?

CHAPTER NINE

BOILING FURY

J OAN KEPT A HANDGUN in the truck for emergencies. She'd purchased a safety holster that attached securely beneath the driver's seat and released quickly in an emergency. Tonight, she didn't need the holster. She slipped the gun free and placed it in her lap, the cold metal a comfort against the rising unease in her chest. Her fingers tightened on the steering wheel as she turned the truck to avoid the figure standing in the driveway.

Susan. Carrie's mother.

Joan slammed on the brakes, the truck lurching to a stop as dust swirled around the headlights. She flung open the door, barely aware of leaving the gun on the seat as she jumped out. The cold night air hit her face, and the smell of dry earth filled her nose.

"Is it Carrie?" Joan's voice was sharp, her heart racing as she stared at Susan. It was the first time she'd ever seen her off the Hogg property.

Susan's hand flew to her mouth, her face twisted with fear. The words that tumbled from her lips were incoherent, a garbled mess of sounds. It wasn't even recognizable as English. Her face was also swollen, and a dark bruise was visible even in the moonlight.

"I need you to tell me if Carrie is okay," Joan demanded, stepping forward. She grabbed Susan's trembling hand and pulled it away from her mouth, her fingers brushing against clammy skin. Susan's entire body was shaking. The weakness, the fear, it set Joan's teeth on edge.

"I need help," Susan managed, her voice barely audible between sobs.

Joan's stomach clenched. "Okay, I can help," she said, her tone firm. "Do we need to call an ambulance?"

Joan reached for the outside switch by the door to trigger the security light. The soft click of the light flickering on bathed them in harsh brightness, and Joan finally got a good look at Susan. She was a mess. Her pale blue eyes were blood-shot and rimmed with dark, sunken circles. Her hair, usually pinned back tightly, was frayed and escaping its hold. Her cotton dress was too thin for the cool June evening, hanging loosely around her bony shoulders.

The dark smudges on her legs and dress; were they dirt or blood? Joan blinked. Susan had no shoes. Barefoot on this jagged terrain, just like her daughter. A knot of dread formed in Joan's gut. Whatever had brought her here had to be bad.

"Look, Susan," Joan said slowly, trying to keep her voice steady, "I need to call an ambulance for your daughter. And we need the police. You know this is bigger than me."

Susan shook her head, violently enough that Joan thought she might hurt herself. Her refusal was frantic, her shoulders shaking harder. Joan's mind skimmed through tonight's details, torn dress, dirt or blood caked on her legs. Joan's anger began to bubble up. Enough of this.

"You don't know me," Joan said, taking a step forward, "except through Jeb's eyes, but I care about Carrie. I knew something was wrong the last time I saw her." Joan's voice softened, but her resolve didn't. "I can help, but you need to let me."

Susan kept shaking her head, and Joan's patience snapped. This had gone on long enough. She didn't have time for this helpless dithering.

With a deep breath, Joan walked to Lucy, yanked her keys from the ignition, shoved the gun under the seat, and went back toward the house. As soon as she opened the door, Max bounded out, his whole body vibrating with excitement.

"Yes, yes," Joan muttered as she scratched behind his ears. "You've been a good boy, and you'll get your treat later. Right now, we've got something urgent to handle."

Max barked happily, his stubby tail wagging back and forth, oblivious to the gravity of the situation. Joan glanced toward the road, her eyes narrowing. She didn't trust Jeb not to come here, especially if he discovered Susan missing. He'd managed to bully the neighbors, but not Joan, and this would be the first place he looked. Max sensed her tension and quieted, his ears twitching as he scanned the area.

"He won't hurt you," Joan murmured, glancing back at the woman.

Susan was gone.

Joan's eyes darted around, scanning the dimly lit yard, but Carrie's mother had vanished into the night. Her chest tightened with frustration as she stared into the darkness, but there was no sign of her. No sound.

Shaking her head, Joan strode back to the truck, anger simmering beneath her skin. She was calling the sheriff's department. If Carrie needed an ambulance, they'd send one, and the police would have to deal with Jeb. She wasn't sure if an ambulance would even come this far out, but she had to try.

She gave Max another pet, a little more firmly this time, trying to calm her nerves. The dog looked up at her, his wide eyes tracking her every movement. "Alright, buddy," she muttered, heading for the truck. "Let's get that phone and make a call."

But her phone wasn't there.

Joan's heart skipped a beat as she frantically searched the cup holder and the floorboards. She even shoved her hands between the cushions. Nothing. Susan had taken it.

"Great," Joan muttered, scrubbing a hand over her face. Without the phone, there was no way to call for help from here. She cursed Susan under her breath for good measure. What now?

Max padded over to his favorite scrub bush and lifted his leg. Joan waited, tapping her foot impatiently as he finished his business. She ran through her options. Maybe Max could track Susan, but he'd never been trained for that. Still, he was smart. Maybe...

No. It wasn't worth the risk. The quickest help would come from Deputy Berger. She'd been to his place once, and though it was a bit of a backwoods drive, she figured she could find it again. It would mean passing by the Hogg homestead, but there was no other choice. Berger was her best bet.

She sighed, looking down at Max, who had trotted back to her side, tail no longer wagging. He was now as worried as she was. "Alright," she said, her voice low. "You're coming with me this time."

She grabbed her gun and tucked it back into the safety holster under the seat. If she needed it, she could grab it quickly. She had a bad feeling in her gut, and it wasn't just from Susan's sudden visit. Something was terribly wrong.

"Come on, Max," Joan called as she climbed into the truck. Max leapt into the driver's seat before shifting over to his side. Joan leaned over to roll down the window for him. His tongue lolled, as he stuck his head out.

"You're too much," Joan muttered with a shake of her head as she threw the truck into gear. She traveled to the end of the drive and turned off the property. "This was going to come to a head someday," Joan said aloud, more to herself than to Max. "Now it's here, and I don't know if I'm ready."

Max ignored her, too busy snapping at the wind as it rushed through the open window. The dust kicked up behind them, swirling in the truck's wake, but Joan's mind was elsewhere.

"That poor child," she muttered. "I might not like her mother's weakness, but she's been abused too. It's gone on long enough."

The adrenaline buzzing through her veins made her hands tremble on the steering wheel. Four years of living with the Hoggs as neighbors had all led to this. Four years of hell.

Joan was still muttering to herself, lost in thought, when Lucy's windshield exploded with a sharp crack, and Joan barely had time to react. She swerved off the dirt road, the truck careening into the scrub.

Her heart pounded as she fought for control.

CHAPTER TEN

EXPLOSIVE WRATH

J OAN'S TRUCK CAREENED DOWN a steep hill, bouncing along as its worn suspension creaked with every dip and rise in the uneven terrain. The engine growled with a deep, throaty rumble. Dust kicked up behind them, and she could barely make out the shadows of the men standing in front of the Hoggs' drive. The tires crunched over loose rocks, roots, and low shrubs. The frame rattled with a steady clank and thud, the metal body groaning as it strained, rattling Joan's teeth. The muffler let out a low, vibrating hum as she shifted gears. The engine growled louder as she picked up speed. Joan's stomach tightened after another shotgun blast. Thankfully, it missed. She switched off the headlights and did everything she could not to tap her brakes, thankful for the cloudy night sky that was currently shading the moonlight.

"Hold on, baby, hold on," she whispered as the cab rattled and shook.

Joan kept a white-knuckled grip on the wheel, her body jerking with every jolt and dip. The tires bounced and slid unpredictably over the uneven ground, but Joan knew her truck, and if she hit nothing too large, Lucy could do this. She turned into larger slides to gain traction. The crushing sound of bushes taken out by the heavy-duty grill filled the cab. Lucy never wavered.

Joan braced herself, knowing that any moment could bring a hard drop or sudden impact. Heart pounding, adrenaline flooded her system, each bump amplified her fear.

Max's growls turned to ferocious barking, which let Joan know he hadn't been hit by the slug. She would check him for glass when they were out of danger.

Joan's heart pumped so hard she thought it would fly from her chest. She kept her speed up and trusted that Lucy would make it. She hoped she was far enough away that they could no longer strike the tires.

Her mind filled with every threat Jeb Hogg made over the years. He had always planned to kill her. She'd figured that out after she testified in court. She knew this day would come, and she wouldn't go down without a fight. The thought of killing his boys, even in self-defense, had weighed on her. Now all of Jeb's sons were over eighteen, and she didn't have those reservations. If they came for her, she would fight back.

Joan's worry turned to Susan and Carrie. Where were they? Without her cell phone, Joan had no way to communicate with anyone.

Strike that. She had internet, which meant she could email.

If she made it back to the house, she would email a 911 to the neighbors she'd connected with. Hopefully, someone would call the sheriff.

Poor Lucy spilled down another large ravine and tilted sideways, going onto two wheels before she righted herself with a heavy jolt and continued forward. They bumped up another rise and came out on the road again. Joan pushed her boot to the floorboard to get Lucy moving as she switched gears while the old faithful engine groaned.

A list ran through Joan's head. She had to turn on the router and the computer to send the emails before the Hoggs invaded her property. She rounded the last corner too fast and skidded several feet until the tires grabbed the road.

"We need to get in the house quickly," she yelled at Max, putting her arm out to stop him flying forward as she slammed on the brakes.

It did little more than wrench her shoulder. Somehow, he managed to stay in the seat with only a small chest bump against the dash. She jumped out, grabbed the shotgun off its rack, and ran toward the front door with Max right behind her. Her fingers shook as she unlocked the security screen, the main lock, and then the deadbolt. She ran inside and closed the doors behind them, securing the locks again. She needed to use the damn bathroom and should have done it before she even headed to Deputy Berger's place. Maybe he heard the gunfire, and he was on his way.

The travel trailer Deputy Berger lived in was nothing to rave about. He'd come out on the losing side of his second divorce and bought his property with the money he had left. After saving enough, he added a well. The good thing was his trailer walls were thin, and sound carried out here. Where it came from was the problem, but with the Hoggs around, it would be the first place she would look. Joan wasn't sure if the deputy was that smart.

She ran to the bathroom and didn't bother closing the door. Max didn't follow, which was the reason she usually shut it. When she finished, she headed to the router. With the flick of a switch, it was on.

Max growled at the front door.

Hoggs.

If no one came to help, they would enter her home quickly. She'd thought about it before. She had grates on the windows and security doors, but shotguns, especially loaded with slugs, would make holes large enough to eventually get through.

When she bought the property, there was a hidden shelter below ground. Joan had her greenhouse built on top of it and made a fake garden box that swung away to expose the door. This was done long before the Hogg family moved in, and she used it as a root cellar, but it was equipped for emergencies too.

"Come on, boy, it's time to move," she said and heard the truck coming as soon as the words left her lips.

She ran to the back door and quickly unlocked it and the security screen. With hands that shook worse than before, she took the time to relock. If they thought she was inside, they would spend their time getting in. Help had to come.

Max followed at her side; his low grumbles matched how she felt. Joan threw open the greenhouse door and ran in, closing it behind them. She heard male voices in the distance and knew they would circle the house within a few minutes. The planter box had a latch attached at the back corner. She slid it free and swung the entire box until she saw the darkened entrance.

"Come on, down you go," she ordered Max. The stairs wouldn't fit them both, and she had to swing the planter back into place and lock the hatch. It took a few seconds before she was beside Max again.

"We made it," she whispered while running her fingers through his fur before she buried her entire face in the ruff of his neck.

He growled.

"Shush," she said in a low voice and pulled him closer. He made a small whining noise then went quiet.

Shotgun blasts filled the night, and even in her shelter, it was loud. Jeb and his sons yelled threats and curses as they blasted the house. Max's chest rumbled slightly, but no sound came out.

"You fuckin' bitch. We're gonna string you up," Jeb yelled.

Life had thrown Joan too many setbacks, and she was done with Jeb Hogg and all he represented. Carrie and Susan deserved better. When Willow came home, she deserved more than to have those vile men living next to them.

Fury filled Joan's brain, and a wildfire ignited in her chest, spreading through her body. Her muscles tightened, and her pulse pounded like a drum in her ears. Joan's thoughts became laser-focused on Jeb Hogg and her endless dislike, drowning out everything else. Her mind was hijacked by a single, overwhelming emotion, blazing hot, relentless, and impossible to ignore.

Rage.

Her vision narrowed, her breath came in shallow, rapid bursts as the fury amplified. A storm of vengeance took root, swirling and demanding action; anything to release the boiling pressure inside.

Her hold on Max grew tighter as rational thought faded into the background, replaced by the overwhelming need to stop Jeb Hogg and his sons. An almost primal urge to kill consumed her. It wasn't just the Hoggs. What the legal system had done to Willow, an innocent child, added to her fury. The fury grew hotter with every curse coming from Jeb and his boys. They'd brought dogs too, and their growling made it crystal clear.

Killing Jeb Hogg was the only answer.

CHAPTER ELEVEN

INFERNAL HATRED

CRIES OF "OLD LADY" echoed through the night, their voices sharp and mocking.

Their next words sent a chill through her bones.

"Come out, come out, wherever you are." The boys were taunting her.

She winced as they entered the greenhouse, knocking over pots and shattering glass. Their dogs growled and barked; the sounds amplified in the buried shelter. Joan's lips pressed into a grim line. Stupid Hoggs. They didn't realize their dogs weren't barking for fun, they were alerting to something.

Joan's grip tightened on her shotgun. The handgun on her hip was loaded too. If they found the shelter's entrance, she wouldn't hesitate in defending herself and Max.

"She ain't here," one of the Hoggs said.

"She's somewhere, and we'll find her. That bitch knows what happened to Carrie. She and that dog of hers need to die."

The name hit Joan like a hammer: *Carrie.*

Her breath caught. What had they done to that poor, innocent child? Anger simmered beneath her skin, swelling with every cruel word they spoke.

"She took that dog of hers into the night. We'll get her, and no one will find the body," another voice said, his tone casual, as though discussing nothing more than a chore. "Are we gonna burn the house?"

"Da says that'll bring the cops. We gotta kill her first, then dump her body in the house before we light it up."

"What if someone hears the gunfire?"

"The deputies are at the high school football game. Most of the people out here are too. The rest'll mind their own damn business."

Joan's heart sank. They were right. Deputy Berger and her neighbors wouldn't be home for hours. Small town football was the highlight of the year. Joan had never attended, but Deputy Berger invited her once. Her answer hadn't been pleasant.

"What if Da's wrong, you dumb shit?"

A thud and a muffled groan followed. "Ow! Stop that."

"Da's pissed worse than I've ever seen. He'll kill us if we mess up. Just do what he says."

Their voices faded, and the barking and gunfire died with them. Joan sat in the silence, her heart pounding. She clenched her jaw. Her neighbors, her so-called community, weren't coming.

"Joan Morgan," Jeb's voice cut through the night, "we're gonna find you no matter where you hide."

A scream pierced the air. "That damn dog bit me! Get him off! Get him off!"

Ferocious growls reverberated through the underground shelter, followed by a high-pitched yelp.

"Shut your hole!" Jeb bellowed. "There's something wrong with him. I'll take the brindle, but we're leaving the others. If that old bitch comes back, the dogs'll tear her apart."

Joan hadn't thought it could get worse, but it had.

"Grab everything worth takin', and we're getting outta here," Jeb shouted.

For another thirty minutes, Joan endured the sounds of her life being ripped apart. Shattering glass and things being destroyed filled the night. Then came the relief of an engine starting, the truck rumbling away.

She allowed herself to breathe slowly, but dread crept back quickly. Jeb's dogs were still out there. The destruction they'd left behind was bad enough, but now she had to deal with animals trained to kill.

"This won't be easy," she whispered to Max.

They couldn't stay in the shelter. If Jeb and his boys came back and got serious about searching, they'd find her.

"I can't shoot the dogs," she murmured, stroking Max's head. "They'll hear the shots."

She was stalling for time, trying to piece together a plan. How many dogs had they left? Five, maybe eight? A truck bed could hold that many, even with two boys riding back there.

Max could protect her, but against more than two dogs? She didn't want to find out. He'd never been in a real fight, but Jeb's dogs were bred and trained for one thing: violence.

Her gaze shifted to the shotgun's stock, then to the shovel propped against the wall. Both would work, but neither felt right. She didn't want to kill any dog, but if it came down to her or them, she'd do what she had to.

"This is life or death, Max," she said, steeling herself.

Sliding back the bolt, she prepared to push the planter aside. She paused, listening. Silence. She took a deep breath and moved the planter.

The cold night air hit her face as she took the first step out, but Max darted ahead, his body tense with purpose. Joan gritted her teeth as her knees creaked while climbing out.

A burst of growls erupted from the opposite side of the house.

Max had found the enemy.

Chapter Twelve

Wrath Cometh

JOAN SHAKILY GRABBED THE flashlight from where it was mounted on the side of the garden door, flipped it on, and walked toward the growls. Max and another dog faced each other, their low snarls filling the night. Their bodies were tightly coiled, and neither backed down.

She used the flashlight to scan the area, looking for the other dogs. None were in sight, but the hair on the back of her neck stood on end. They could come from anywhere. Rage or not, Joan knew she was in over her head. She also knew someone would die tonight, and she didn't want it to be her.

She tilted the flashlight toward the dog facing Max. He was large, but that's not what drew her attention as she stepped closer. White foam bubbled from his jaws, and long tendrils of saliva swung from side to side as he growled. He took a strange, shaky step to the side and lowered his nose, then raised it. He followed this by shaking his head in an odd manner. Suddenly, his entire body trembled like he was having some sort of seizure. For some odd reason, it reminded Joan of the last time she saw Carrie. The dog's crazed eyes jerked around and landed on her for a moment before they returned to Max. His bared fangs and tight, rippling muscles showed the fight was already on.

Joan's thoughts went into overdrive as her focus snapped back and forth between the two. Adrenaline coursed through her body. Time seemed to stretch; each second felt impossibly long as her mind frantically tried to grasp the pieces of the puzzle. The pulse in her temples kept a pounding rhythm, her heartbeat thundering in her ears as the world blurred and sharpened in alternating waves of panic and focus.

Every sensory detail felt magnified. Sights, sounds, and smells bombarded her brain, distracting it from the crucial task at hand. Joan grasped at fragmented thoughts, scanning through past knowledge, trying to make sense of what she saw. The answer was just out of reach, tangled in fear and confusion.

Then, suddenly, she had a mental snap, like the gears finally locked into place and the information came together in a flash of clarity as the fog lifted.

Carrie's trembling and jerky motions. The foam at the dog's mouth.

Rabies.

Suddenly, the rabid dog sprang at Max. Guttural snarls cut the air, and their jaws snapped at each other before they collided. The force of the impact sent them rolling head over tail. They recovered instantly, twisting and turning as they tried to gain a grip on the other. The strange dog did a crazy lurch sideways again.

Joan didn't think. She charged in, her shotgun raised over her head like a wild woman. Max backed off; seemingly like they planned it. She swung downward with everything she had, striking the dog's back. He yelped, then snapped in her direction as he turned to lunge at her. Max grabbed him by the side of his throat and began shaking with enough force to lift the other dog off its feet. There was a short struggle before the dog's body went limp. Max held on as his deep growls dwindled.

Panting and trying to regain her equilibrium, Joan considered what she knew about rabies. Not much. No one spoke or even thought about rabies anymore. What she remembered came from her childhood over sixty years before. Foaming at the mouth and hydrophobia were the obvious signs. Then she remembered that once outward signs of rabies appeared, there was no cure. Was it still that way?

Carrie.

She was dead. No, Joan couldn't accept that without seeing it for herself. Carrie and her mother had to be alive.

What if all of Jeb's dogs were in some stage of the disease? There had to be over a hundred of them. She doubted he ever vaccinated any of them for anything.

Fear caught up to her, and an iron grip squeezed her chest, pulling tighter with every breath. Her heart pounded so violently it had to find a way out. Sweat trickled down her back, and her hands trembled as she gazed into the night, feeling the other dogs watching and waiting. Every nerve in her body screamed for her to hide and escape what she knew was out there.

Her mind cycled through worst-case scenarios, amplifying every possible horror until even the most remote possibility felt inevitable. Mental whispers were drowned out by the roar of anxiety. Time warped, slowing down so that every second led up to the moment of choice. Her stomach twisted into knots.

Willow floated in her mind, sweet precious child. No, not Willow, Carrie. Joan's confusion blended their images inside her head. Her heart couldn't tell one from the other.

Slowly, reason returned, and the fog of fear lifted. A rabid dog had bitten Max. It or another infected dog had bitten one of Jeb's sons.

Joan had no idea what the rabies protocol was if a dog had its shots other than confinement. She knew she shouldn't touch the dead animal. She had to get Max away from it so she could clean his wounds.

Jeb could deal with his kid. Joan's concern was for her best friend.

"Good boy, Max. Come." She hit her palm against the side of her leg. Max turned in her direction, his jaws still clamped on the other dog's throat. He whined, and she called him again. "Max, come."

His mouth opened. There was a soft thud when the body hit the dirt. Max walked to her side, his eyes glued to hers. Joan went to her knees. He pushed his entire body into her, almost toppling her over.

"You're such a good boy," she told him softly as she ran her shaky hands over his fur. She probably shouldn't touch him either, but she didn't care. She let the fear go. It could and most likely would come back, but she would face it.

Max's front leg was wet. She lifted her hand away and knew it was blood. "Okay, boy, we need to go inside so I can see if the blood is yours or his. You did good," she assured him. He followed her to the house, her hand on his neck steadying them both.

Joan turned the corner of the house and sucked in a deep breath. Lucy. She walked around the truck. There were four punctured tires and windshield damage. It was fixable, but it ramped up her anger to rage again. She took several deep breaths. Lucy was a truck. She could be fixed. It didn't matter. Joan had to look away.

The front security door on her house and the main door were shot off the hinges. Items from inside were dragged out and littered the ground. Most of it destroyed. Joan carefully stepped over items and moved around larger pieces of furniture to get inside.

It was worse.

Bags of food storage were torn open, and cans tossed everywhere. They'd smashed a bottle of olive oil. A slick, glossy film seemed to cover everything. It was too much to deal with, and the mess wasn't a priority, it was just something to keep her rage up.

Gazing around, she realized she couldn't close the front door behind her for security. If the Hoggs or the dogs came back, she would be in trouble. This had to be quick.

Max followed her into the bathroom this time. She flipped the light switch, but it didn't work. Jeb or his sons had most likely pulled the wires out of the fuse box. She propped the flashlight on the counter and turned on the water. She took a large towel from the cabinet and wet it before resituating the flashlight on the toilet seat so she could see Max.

"This might hurt," she told him after she sat down on the floor. Her fingers still trembled.

He had a small flap of skin on his snout. It wasn't bleeding, but it was a puncture wound caused by a bite. Max stayed perfectly still as she examined every inch of him. She cleaned his fur with soap and water, then poured peroxide over the actual bites she found. Thankfully, most of the blood belonged to the other dog. She ran her fingers through Max's fur one last time to be sure she hadn't missed anything. Leaning in, she took a moment to breathe in his scent.

Joan needed this, even knowing she didn't have much time. They could die tonight. It was a very real possibility. After a sharp shake of her head, she moved, grabbed the flashlight, and faced the mirror.

There were deep lines etched into her forehead, and her eyebrows were drawn together in a tight furrow. The crow's feet and deeper shadows around her eyes reflected exhaustion. Her lips pressed into a thin, taut line, and the corners of her mouth pulled downward as she stared at herself. Her once-brown hair had been straight, and now it was a mass of white curls that she'd allowed to grow because getting it cut was a pain in the butt.

She leaned in and stared into her hazel eyes. Wrath and determination stared back. Joan had never killed a person. Before her son-in-law, she'd never considered that she could. She hadn't been there for her daughter Sammy. She wasn't there for Willow until it was too late. It could already be too late for Carrie, and Joan refused to think about that possibility. It was time to fight back. She should have stopped her son-in-law. She'd buried her head in the sand, but she knew the signs of abuse, and it started with control. Neither Willow nor Carrie deserved the life they were born into. Joan was done minding her own business when a child's life was on the line.

Her attention turned to Max, and she crouched down beside him. She might lose her best friend tonight. She didn't think she would have survived Jeb Hogg this long if it weren't for Max.

"I need your help," she said. "It's Carrie. We need to find her. Her mom too. I can't do it alone, and this is dangerous." He stared back, intelligent brown eyes telling her he would do whatever she asked. He whined and pushed his head into her leg.

The Hoggs abused their dogs. Joan had taken more pictures of their atrocities the year before. The sheriff's department, after several lawsuits filed by Jeb, stayed clear of the family. Her new evidence did nothing.

She took a deep breath and allowed the fear to fade even more. A child's life was at stake, and this ended tonight. Maybe there were advances in battling rabies that she didn't know about, and Carrie could be saved. Joan would hold onto the thought and do whatever it took.

She stood among her damaged things that meant little right now. Her thoughts tumbled around what had to be done and how to do it. She would take the fight to them. It was the only way Carrie and Susan had a chance. Help wouldn't arrive for hours, and she couldn't wait.

Joan was in excellent shape despite her age. The deep hatred she felt for Jeb pulsed within her brain. She allowed the rage to build further. It would give her the strength to do what had to be done.

Jeb had added a large metal barn for the dogs about two years before. She could no longer see the daily abuse that had burned into her soul. Deputy Berger actually warned her to stay away from the Hoggs. His warning hadn't stopped her. Due to her occasional night surveillance operations, she knew their property almost as well as she knew hers.

Joan pushed a wisp of hair from her face and spotted one of her ball caps on the floor. After twisting her hair onto the crown of her head, she pulled the cap over it. The dark color would help keep her white hair hidden.

The house no longer felt like home. It had been violated. She knew it could be cleaned, but it didn't help the sadness at seeing so many of her things destroyed. She reminded herself to focus. Carrie was all that mattered now.

Joan's closet suffered the least damage. They'd dragged some stuff out, but most of her things were still inside. She located a long-sleeved black pullover and black cargo pants with plenty of pockets that she liked to hike in.

The rack of knives she kept on the kitchen counter was gone. She had a hunting knife in the root cellar that would work. She also had bear spray if they hadn't found it. She'd ordered the stuff after her first mountain lion sighting. She went into the bathroom and pulled the can from the back corner of the cabinet. She didn't care that Dale Berger warned her she would spray herself if she used it. The deputy could go to hell.

A twelve-by-twelve strong box was in the back of her closet, hidden behind a stack of clothes, and they hadn't found it. She carried it with her when she went for the hunting knife.

She left the strong box behind. Deputy Berger knew about the underground hideaway. Everything Willow would need was in the box. Joan didn't like the deputy, but she had no choice but to trust him if she didn't survive. She probably should have been nicer to him through the years.

Joan didn't think about death as she prepared. Her life no longer mattered. She thought of the suffering they'd put the dogs through. She thought of the bruises on Carrie and her mother. With crystal clearness, Joan knew it was Jeb Hogg and his sons or Carrie and Susan.

Joan had been on this path for a long time.

CHAPTER THIRTEEN

HOGG HELL DAY THREE

BY THE TIME JEB and his sons returned home, his throat burned with a fire that wouldn't ease. Sweat dripped from every pore, soaking his clothes, and a sour odor clung to him; a stench he couldn't escape. He staggered into the kitchen and grabbed another jug of water, desperate to quench his thirst. As soon as he raised it to his mouth, his throat seized. He gagged and spat the water across the room, coughing and choking violently.

Saliva pooled in his mouth, thick and uncontrollable. His hands shook as he wiped it away, a cold dread sinking in. Then it hit him like a thunderclap.

His bitch of a wife was poisoning him.

"Where are you, Susan?" he bellowed, his voice cracking with rage.

"Da, what's wrong?" one of his sons asked, stepping forward hesitantly.

"Get the fuck away from me, or I'll kill you too!" Jeb roared, storming past him, his breath ragged as he searched the house for his wife.

He headed for the bedroom first, but Susan wasn't there. He knew her hiding spots. Swinging open Carrie's closet door, he found her crouched inside, trembling.

"There you are!" He grabbed a fistful of her hair and yanked her out, her screams cutting through the air like a knife.

"Shut the hell up!" he shouted, slamming his hand across her face. Her head snapped to the side, and her cries turned to whimpers. He struck her again, this time with his fist, the blow landing hard against her temple. Her body crumpled, but he wasn't done.

Jeb dragged her up by her hair, her feet barely brushing the floor. She clawed at his hands, gasping for breath. "What are you poisoning me with?" he growled, his face inches from hers, his spit flecking her skin.

Her wide, terrified eyes said she couldn't answer even if she wanted to. He shook her violently, slamming her head against the wall with each shout. "Tell me! Answer me, goddamn it!"

Susan's eyes rolled back, and her body went limp. He let go, and she collapsed in a heap. Her skull cracked against the floor with a sickening thud.

Jeb stood over her, his chest heaving, then kicked her ribs with enough force to send her sliding across the floor. Her body didn't move. He didn't care.

His arm itched furiously. He clawed at it, tearing open a wound he didn't remember getting. Blood oozed from the jagged scratches, and he stared at it, trying to make sense of why it was there.

"Where's Carrie?" he shouted, his voice echoing through the house as he stormed out of the room. "Where is that bitch?"

His sons stood frozen by the front door, their faces pale.

"You heard me! Where is she?"

"Da?" one of them stammered, taking a cautious step back.

Jeb's eyes darted toward the shotgun leaning against the wall. He snatched it up, his hands gripping it tightly.

"Where's Carrie?" he demanded again.

His oldest son swallowed hard and answered, "Carrie's gone, Da. We buried her a mile from here."

For a fleeting moment, Jeb's mind cleared. He remembered. He had beaten Carrie to death, hadn't he? Yes, her battered body, limp and lifeless. The memory was vivid.

But then he saw her.

She stood outside the window, her face pale and her eyes staring straight at him.

"She's not dead!" he screamed, his voice raw. He raised the shotgun, aiming at her apparition. Without hesitation, he pulled the trigger.

The window shattered, glass exploding outward as the deafening blast filled the room. The force sent him stumbling back against the wall, his ears ringing.

When his vision cleared, she was gone.

Jeb dropped to his knees, his body trembling uncontrollably. He tried to catch his breath, but it was useless. His throat burned, his muscles twitched, and his thoughts fragmented into incoherent chaos.

He glanced around the room. His boys had disappeared.

Chapter Fourteen

Hogg Flesh, Hogg Blood

JOAN THOUGHT ABOUT TAKING Max's leash but decided against it. If things turned as bad as she expected, the ability to run away could save him. His collar was thick leather and would protect his throat, so it stayed on.

She found one of her metal water bottles and washed it. The thing fit perfectly in her side leg pocket. She highly doubted any of Jeb's dogs were friendly, but she loaded another pocket with Max's kibble. If a dog showed signs of rabies, she had no trouble putting it down, but it was easier to picture harming Jeb over his dogs. In Joan's current mood, she would do whatever it took.

She dug through her medical supplies and stuffed two stretch bandages into a pocket. She also grabbed matches before upending things on her floor to find any other item she thought she might need. Jeb said that burning down her house would bring the authorities. Burning his would do the same, and she placed two lighters and a small box of matches she used to light her wood-burning stove into a separate pocket. Joan holstered her handgun after being sure it had one in the chamber ready to fire. She didn't own shotgun slugs, but the buckshot would do a lot of damage and cover a wider area. She mentally listed everything she could possibly need and added another flashlight that had twine wrapped around the handle and might come in handy.

She was ready.

"Let's go find Carrie," she told Max. He licked her hand before he took off and ran outside. He was halfway to the wash when she caught up to him. He hiked with Joan, and he knew where Carrie lived.

Joan realized Max had known something was wrong with his young friend. She had no idea if he scented it or if it was Carrie's odd behavior, but he knew. He'd warned her about danger before, and she needed to pay closer attention when he acted strangely. If she had understood, none of this might have happened.

She shut down her feelings of guilt.

Clouds traveled above her, offering glimpses of the full moon. Its glow allowed her to see without using her flashlight most of the time. There was a section on her property where high canyon walls blocked the moonlight, and she had to turn the flashlight on so she didn't break a leg. She shut it off as soon as she could see again.

The hike gave her time to think. Her city handyman ability was little more than changing out a lightbulb. Now she knew about solar energy, wells, electrical wiring, voltage, and amperage. Most of the knowledge came from YouTube videos. All of it was for Willow. Joan wanted her to have a place to call her own when she got out of prison. Jeb had destroyed the safety net Joan had built for her granddaughter, and one way or another, it ended tonight.

Would Willow understand why Joan was taking on Jeb? She felt Willow would eventually forgive her if she didn't survive. Her granddaughter had to be safe so she could live her entire life out here if she wanted to.

Fifteen minutes into the hike, a low rumbling growl came from the bushes. Max's fur stood on end. He answered the threat with his own low rumble. They were too close to the Hoggs' place for Joan to turn on the flashlight or fire her weapon. A dog fight could alert them too. The bushes rustled, and her heart pounded.

A reddish-brown dog stood between Joan and her rescue operation. Another one, black this time, came from the opposite side. They snarled at each other before turning crazed eyes on Joan and Max.

Rabies. The word swelled inside her head again. She lifted her shotgun like a baseball bat. The dogs attacked without warning. Max rammed the lighter one. The black dog made it past him and launched himself at Joan. She swung. The shotgun hit him with a solid thunk, but it didn't even slow him down. Joan fell backward on impact. Her adrenaline was too high to feel pain. He grabbed her leg below the knee, his teeth sinking deep.

It almost felt surreal.

The stabbing ache was relentless. The pressure was far stronger than she expected. It felt as if he were crushing bone.

For a moment, panic took over. The realization of the attack was suffocating. Her instincts screamed to defend herself, overriding the pain to snap her from the paralyzing fight-or-flight decision that was too late. Joan lifted her upper body and punched the dog's head with her right fist. It did nothing. She remembered the knife right as her leg was tugged, pulling her away from the other dogs.

She could hear them fighting. Max had to survive.

Suddenly, the knife was in her hand, and she drove it into the side of the dog's neck over and over. He didn't whimper or cry. His teeth stayed clamped on her leg, biting deep. He wouldn't die, and Joan had no idea how much more she could take.

Suddenly, Max was there, his fury precisely what was needed. The injured dog didn't stand a chance. Max rammed him with the force of a sledgehammer, and he released her leg. Joan sank into the earth beneath her, hitting soft sand. She gasped for breath. Burning pain shot through her leg. After the dog stopped moving, Max crawled to her side and whined softly. Sniffing her face, he let her know he was okay as he assured himself of the same. She lifted one arm and touched his bloody muzzle.

"Give me a minute," she whispered as she took a mental snapshot of her injuries. She bent her bitten leg slowly. It was still attached, and the thought made her smile despite what she had just been through. "Of course it was attached," she chided herself softly.

"There are more dogs," she whispered to Max. "I need to get up." The words were for her this time.

She was in the middle of the wash, which was about twenty-five yards across. Too far to drag herself to one side or the other. She dug in her pockets for the bandages she'd thankfully brought. After a few minutes, she sat up. Gently, she pushed Max away.

"I'm okay, you big lug. Thank you."

She knew that looking at the wounds was not a good idea. She used one ace bandage to wrap around her upper calf, pressing the pant material into the bites. It hurt, but she had to find Carrie and her mother. This couldn't stop her. She wiped tears from her eyes and tried to shove the pain into its own box.

"Some tough gal I am," she said to Max. He whined. "I'll look at you next, but I doubt I can do much." He had to be okay.

Joan had no idea how long she stayed there. Max had more blood in his fur and a nasty bite on his front leg, though it didn't seem to faze him yet. Her biggest test was getting to her feet and taking a step. The dog had shaken its head while clamping down on her leg, and she knew it was more than a simple bite. There was likely muscle and tendon damage. Still, she took that first step and then another. She loosened the bandage slightly because her toes felt numb.

After a few shaky steps, she could put all her weight on the injured one, pain be damned. Her shotgun rested a few feet away, and she picked it up.

"You coming with me?" she asked Max.

The look in his eyes gave her more strength. He would protect Carrie just like he did her.

She could walk, but the injury slowed her progress. She also stopped every few minutes and listened to the night noises. There were more dogs on the prowl.

Her injured leg would make climbing the ridge difficult. She would crawl if needed. Nothing would stop her.

"We're doing this slowly," she told Max when she could see the jagged rocky hill they had to hike.

It took twice as long as usual to make it to the top. Finally, she could see the Hogg homestead below. She made her way to the bushes she'd used before to get her photos. She always took the time to scrub her footprints away with a branch before she left. This time it didn't matter, but the hiding spot was a good area to look at the house and make a solid plan once she knew where the men were.

Going to her stomach, she slid through the dirt and positioned herself. She rested the binoculars beside her before she called Max to join her. It took him a fraction of the time it took her to slide in. Max panted softly, and the sound comforted her. Joan lifted the field glasses and scanned the area.

The campfire burned in the pit like it always had. With the unending supply of shaggy-bark wood littered throughout the ranch, Jeb had all the free firewood he needed. Joan resented the fire. Jeb used it to hide his crimes.

She checked the wrapping on her leg. Part of it was wet, but she wasn't in danger of bleeding to death. The thought of rabies freaked her out some. Both the reddish-brown and black dog showed signs. She would get the shots and be okay. Max would stay with her while he was in isolation. She could do this.

After her mental pep talk, she panned the binoculars from barn to house. Nothing moved but the flames in the fire. She did it again from the opposite direction.

Jeb stepped from the shadows into a streak of silver moonlight, his face stony, unreadable. The brindle moved at his side, silent and watchful, muscles tense as if sensing the weight of what was to come. In Jeb's arms, his shotgun rested easily, an extension of his cruelty.

Without warning, he raised the weapon, its muzzle now trained on the worn wooden porch of his home. The movement was swift but decisive, as if every muscle in his body had been preparing for this single act. Joan felt her pulse surge as she searched the dim porch, heart pounding as her gaze fell upon a figure standing there, caught in the starkness of her binocular lens.

It was one of Jeb's sons. His posture was rigid, as if even the slightest twitch might shatter him. The silence of the night split as the shotgun roared, its deafening crack tearing through the stillness, rolling through Joan's ears. In a breathless moment, the figure on the porch seemed to hang suspended. Then, he crumpled. It was as if time had stretched, slowing the brutal descent. The soft glow of the moon caught him as he fell, casting a shadow across the wooden boards.

Joan held her breath. Then, slowly, the echo of the shot faded, swallowed by the night, leaving only the quiet, haunting rustle of the breeze.

Jeb Hogg murdered his own flesh and blood.

Chapter Fifteen

Gone Rabid

Locked in horror, Joan gasped, her hand flying to her mouth as her eyes stayed fixed on the binoculars. Her mind reeled, struggling to comprehend what she'd seen. Her heart pounded so fiercely it seemed to reverberate through her entire body. She blinked hard, half-expecting the insane scene might vanish. But there Jeb stood, alone in the stark moonlight, his hands clutched around the smoking shotgun.

Realizing she'd been holding her breath, Joan exhaled sharply, and a sudden dizziness hit her, sending the world into a brief, sickening whirl. It thankfully didn't last. Her hands shook as she adjusted the binoculars to scan the area again. The darkened house loomed quietly, taunting her with its silence. She strained to see through the thick shadows surrounding the porch, her gaze darting from filthy window to filthy window.

No sign of the other boys? Where was Carrie? Susan?

Her chest tightened with a new kind of dread as she realized that Jeb was the only person in sight. Her ears caught the faintest edge of his voice, rough and sharp as he shouted something into the emptiness, his words just a garbled rumble from her vantage. She tried to make out what he was saying. If she understood, maybe she'd have some explanation for the crazed act she'd witnessed. But the porch remained empty except for the fallen body. Jeb stood like a dark sentinel, his attention somewhere beyond her view.

Even for Jeb Hogg, who had always been known for his simmering temper and erratic outbursts, this was madness on another level. Something in him had snapped. She could feel it as surely as if it were a living, breathing thing in the air between them. And then, with a chill that seemed to creep from her bones to her blood, the realization struck her like a slap.

Jeb Hogg had gone rabid.

Joan's breath caught as Jeb turned, his silhouette looming in the distance as he swung the shotgun toward the darkness. The barrel dipped, only to jerk up again, his movements erratic. Then, another explosion. This time, the blast hit the dirt close enough for her to feel the dull, earthy thud echoing through the ground beneath her. Fifteen feet. Did he know she was out here?

Jeb turned away, facing the driveway, and fired again, this time at nothing but the empty night. Each wild shot only deepened the despair tightening in Joan's stomach. Reflexively, her hand moved to Max's back, fingers threading into his thick fur as she sought comfort in his steady warmth. He leaned into her touch, his quiet presence grounding her even as her thoughts spiraled. She murmured to him, her voice low and unsteady.

"His leash is loose, boy, and the doghouse is empty upstairs. That man is insane."

Hearing herself say it aloud was like crossing some invisible line, one she couldn't retreat from. This was no longer suspicion, the rabies virus now unfolded before her eyes.

She lifted the binoculars again, her gaze darting back to the house. She squinted, desperate to penetrate the darkness beyond and find someone other than Jeb alive.

A dreadful thought took root, one that twisted through her mind like a creeping vine. Why didn't his other sons come running? They would have heard those shots. The blasts had shattered the night. The silence held its own story. Her heart clenched, the horror of it overwhelming, yet the notion refused to let go.

They could all be dead.

Joan's mind raced, torn between the urge to hide and the knowledge that she had to take out Jeb. Rationally, she knew it was safest to hunker down and stay out of sight until the authorities arrived. It could be hours, and lives potentially hung in the balance. Max was a formidable presence at her side, but even he wouldn't be able to protect them if Jeb decided to start firing in her direction again. Besides, she wouldn't turn her back on Carrie.

Just then, Jeb lowered the shotgun, his posture shifting as he turned, looking in her direction. The moonlight caught him, and for a chilling moment, she felt as though he were staring straight into her eyes. Her heartbeat thundered as she forced herself to stay still, swallowing hard so she didn't scream. The brindle walked to his side, its head facing ahead with unsettling calmness, in unspoken obedience to its master. They remained that way, locked in silence, Jeb's figure unmoving. The seconds dragged, each one stretching until she feared she might break beneath the pressure.

Then, at last, he turned and headed toward the barn, the dog following with dutiful silence as they vanished into the interior.

Only then did Joan realize she'd been holding her breath again. She exhaled, the cold air rushing into her lungs, and she took another quick scan of the house. Nothing stirred. The porch lay still.

"I need to look in those windows," she whispered to Max, her voice steadying with the decision. She felt the cold grip of fear seize her again, a wave of panic rising in her chest, but she forced it down. She could not leave an innocent child in the hands of a rabid monster.

Carrie and her mother had to be alive, or this was all for nothing. Even though she knew the odds weren't in the young child's favor, Joan would not lose hope. A shaky plan began forming in her mind. It wasn't much of a plan, truth be told, it barely counted as one, but it was all she had.

"Stay," she whispered firmly, placing her palm in front of Max's nose. He watched her with alert eyes, knowing exactly what she meant. He would hold his ground unless she needed him, their unspoken bond stronger than any words could be.

With one last glance at the barn, she took a breath, steeling herself, and crept toward the house. Her leg was now throbbing steadily. She used the shotgun for support.

Joan crouched low; her breath shallow as she edged closer. Each step seemed magnified in the stillness. The dry vegetation crackled underfoot, each crunch ringing in her ears like the snap of brittle bones, impossibly loud against the quiet night. She winced, pausing to lift the binoculars, scanning the property with renewed caution. Satisfied that the area around the barn remained empty, she veered carefully away from it, jerking her head from barn to house, watching for any sign of Jeb or his dog.

The closer she crept, the worse the state of the property became. Broken furniture, rusted-out appliances, and piles of refuse littered the yard, scattered as if someone had emptied their entire life's junk across the land. Someone had. It was like wading through a minefield of filth. Her nose crinkled as she caught the stench; strong, sour, with a heavy undercurrent of stale urine that clung to the air. She breathed shallowly, wishing she had a scarf or anything to shield her nose. How did they live this way?

Keeping to the darkest shadows, she moved from one rusty, broken-down car to the next, pressing her back against them, ready to bolt if she saw so much as a shadow move. Her mind wandered briefly to the brindle, who posed almost the same danger as Jeb. She kept expecting the dog to materialize out of the dark at any moment.

Joan took another careful step forward when her foot struck something solid, sending her to one knee, causing pain to shoot up her bitten leg. She reached out instinctively, her fingers pressing against something unfamiliar beneath her. Confusion washed over her as her mind struggled to understand what she'd stumbled upon. Her hand brushed against the rough fabric of a pant leg, and dread pooled in her stomach as she felt the unyielding shape of a body beneath her touch.

Her fingers moved almost mechanically up the figure's leg, across the torso, and finally to the neck, where she pressed two trembling fingers against the skin. There was no pulse. Her breath hitched. It had to be one of Jeb's sons.

Still warm.

A mixture of horror and sorrow twisted through her, the reality of it settling into her soul. She swallowed hard, resisting the wave of nausea that threatened to overtake her, then forced herself to focus, to stay sharp.

A faint whisper startled Joan, cutting through the night. She gasped, spinning to locate the source of the plea. It came again, softer now, barely audible over the quiet squeak of an old pile of metal about fifty feet away. A few seconds later, she tracked the sound to the porch.

Rising quickly, she dashed from the cover of the junked truck to the steps, her gaze fixing on the figure sprawled at the porch's edge. It was the son Jeb shot, lying on his side, slumped against the rough wood. Darkness seeped from beneath him, the blood mingling with the dirt covering the boards.

His breathing was shallow and strained, each rasp catching in his throat. The sight filled her with horrible urgency. She knelt by his side, her voice low but desperate. "What happened?"

The young man's gaze remained unfocused, clouded by pain and shock. "Da?" he croaked, the single word laced with a raw, pleading confusion.

She leaned closer, her voice gentle. "It's Joan, your neighbor. Where are Carrie and your mother?"

For a brief second, his eyes flickered toward her, and she thought she saw a spark of recognition. His fingers moved, finding her sleeve, and clutched it with a strength that surprised her, his hand shaking. "Ma?" he whispered, the word barely escaping his lips.

"Where is your ma?" she pressed, urgency sharpening her tone.

He swallowed, his gaze unfocused once again, but then his head moved, and his chin lifted just slightly. When he met her eyes, a hollow, resigned look settled over his face. "Dead," he exhaled, his last word escaping in a long sigh as his head drooped. A tremor ran through his body, his hand slackening on her sleeve before it slipped, and he went utterly still.

She found his wrist, pressing into his pulse point with a futile hope. Nothing.

The word—*dead*—echoed in her mind, an impossible reality she couldn't yet let sink in. Susan, gone? Her heart seized with grief and disbelief, her mind veering immediately to Carrie. If her mother was dead, then where had Carrie gone? Her gaze flickered across the dark yard, scanning the silent, hollow structure of the barn in the distance. She caught the sound of a low whine, almost imperceptible, followed by a faint growl. The dogs. Some had to be inside the barn with Jeb.

Pushing aside the tight grip of fear gnawing at her resolve, Joan clenched her jaw. Standing, she took one last glance at the porch and the lifeless form of Jeb's son. She moved toward the front door. She couldn't waste another second looking through the windows, which was her original plan. Carrie could be inside.

The door creaked open, and a foul stench hit her instantly, more concentrated than the yard, thick and suffocating, tinged with the acrid odor of decay. She forced herself to breathe shallowly, resisting the urge to cover her nose. She took a tentative step forward, her eyes straining to adjust. There was no one in the front part of the house. She had to go down the hallway. Fingers shaking, she opened the first door on the left. She could see nothing and took a chance by turning on the flashlight.

Mice scurried away. There were two inches of droppings along the floorboard. A galvanized metal bucket had a toilet lid on top of it. The smell was worse than the night Max got sprayed by a skunk. She quickly turned off her flashlight and closed the door. Poor Carrie had been forced to live in this disgusting filth.

She took a few steps and opened the next door. A bunk bed was against the wall, and a full-sized mattress lay on the floor. Other than beds and clothing, garbage littered the empty room. There was a single closet. She looked inside and saw several dresses belonging to Carrie.

Joan pushed open the final door at the end of the hallway, feeling a strange, prickling unease settle over her. Unlike the other rooms, which reeked of abuse that happened within, this one held an unnerving stillness, an unnatural quiet that sent a chill down her spine. Shadows thickened in the corners, leaving only a narrow path of dim light to the bed. She took a few cautious steps forward, her gaze drawn to the figure lying upon it.

Susan.

Joan's heart thundered in the suffocating silence. Susan's eyes were open, wide and glassy, fixed on something Joan couldn't see, as if she'd glimpsed into another realm in her final moments. Her hands were crossed on her chest. Blood covered her face and matted her hair.

The heaviness in Joan's chest grew, a sharp ache that settled like a weight on her ribs, compressing her breath. Time seemed to warp, stretching out, as she stood rooted to the spot.

Susan's skin was a pallid, waxen gray, her limbs unnaturally still, her body arranged almost like a forgotten doll left to gather dust. Oddly, it was her feet, though. Bare and filthy, smudged with dirt and grime that seemed to strike Joan's sense of injustice the most. Something about the sight made her rage spike. Susan had gone to her house barefoot to get away. This small indignity stood out amid all this horror. Did she return for Carrie?

Joan absorbed every detail, each one twisting her tighter, until finally her mind screamed at her to move, to remember that she was still in danger.

A wave of nausea suddenly swept over her. She closed her eyes for a moment, steeling herself against it, forcing down the bile that threatened to rise. She couldn't afford to fall apart now, not with Carrie's whereabouts still unknown, not with the looming threat that Jeb could return at any moment.

CHAPTER SIXTEEN

RELENTLESS VENGEANCE

THE THOUGHT OF CARRIE snapped Joan from her trance, pulling her back to the grim present. She quickly scanned every corner of the dimly lit room, her gaze lingering on each shadow. Relief should have washed over Joan at not finding Carrie's body, but instead, a thicker dread settled like a heavy cement block on her chest. The uncertainty was worse. Carrie was still missing, most likely dead, and that was somehow harder to bear. If there was even the smallest chance the girl was alive, Joan had to try.

A sharp, angry shout tore through the silence. "I'll kill you, you damned mutt." Jeb's voice bellowed from just outside the bedroom window, thick with malice. A gunshot cracked the air, sharp and jarring.

Joan's heart leapt. Max? She ducked low, instinct kicking in, and half-crawled toward the bedroom door, careful to keep her movements silent. The hallway stretched out before her, dark and filled with looming shadows. She stood and slipped the shotgun strap from her shoulder, bringing the gun to the ready. She couldn't lose Max too; she had to be sure he was safe.

Edging toward the back door she'd noted in the living area, Joan steadied her breathing. The door was unlocked. She slipped outside, her movements a blend of caution and urgency. Cold night air prickled her skin, carrying with it the unmistakable scent of damp earth and fear. Somewhere nearby, a dog's howl cut through the night, wild and anguished. But it wasn't Max. Relief and dread battled in her heart again as she moved carefully toward the side of the house, pressing herself flat against the wall.

Peeking around the corner, Joan saw Jeb's son, a bat raised, preparing to strike the brindle lunging toward him. The animal was faster. It sprang to its hind legs, teeth bared, snapping at his face until the man stumbled. He went down hard, his screams merging with the dog's snarls.

Joan's breath caught. This was her moment to get back to Max before he ran headlong onto the property. She had to move now.

A sound behind her made her stiffen. She turned and froze. Twenty feet away stood Jeb, his shotgun lifted, eyes gleaming with a deranged glee as he moved closer. Joan's mind raced. She tried to back up, stumbling over her own feet in her haste. Her hand shot out to brace herself against the house, fingers scraping against the rough siding.

"I always knew I'd kill you, you crazy bitch." Jeb's voice was low, a poisonous hiss that sliced through the night, punctuated by a laugh that dripped with maniacal satisfaction. Bubbles of spit spilled from between his lips.

He pulled the trigger.

Click.

Nothing happened.

No pain. For a split second, Joan stared, heart still racing. Then, she ran.

"Yeah, run," Jeb shouted after her, his voice dark and taunting. "It'll be more fun to hunt you." A shrill, piercing whistle followed, echoing across the night.

A deep, eager bark rose in response, and dread clawed at Joan's chest. She could hear the dog crashing through the brush, closing in. She pushed herself harder, each step sending jolts through her injured leg. About halfway up the ridge, her legs gave way, lungs burning as she struggled to catch her breath. Precious seconds ticked by before she could force herself to move again, scrambling up the rest of the hill in desperation.

At the top, she stopped short. Max was gone. She searched behind her and there was no sign of the brindle. A hollow feeling spread through her chest as she looked down at her hands, her knuckles white against the shotgun's grip. "I should have shot him," she whispered, the words nearly swallowed by the wind. For a second, the weight of everything pressed down on her, almost breaking her resolve.

"Max," she called softly, straining to listen as the night breathed around her, its quiet sounds carrying a strange, indifferent beauty. A distant owl hooted, and a cool breeze rustled the branches, but no familiar bark answered. She held her breath, focusing. If he'd been near the house, he would have come to her by now.

A shotgun blast shattered the stillness, its echo rolling up the ridge like a thunderclap. Joan threw herself to the ground, heart hammering as she pressed herself into the dirt. The scent of crushed dry grass and dust filled her nose, grounding her in the raw reality of her situation. After a tense moment, she rose slowly, crouching low as she moved into a steady, fast walk. Her leg no longer mattered. She kept her flashlight off. Jeb was close.

Several more shots rang out, from a greater distance but relentless. She wondered if Jeb was shooting wildly, or worse, taking down anyone, or anything, in his path. The thought of Max sent another chill through her.

A noise off to the side caught her attention. Instinctively, she shifted direction, ignoring the dizzying exhaustion that made each step heavier than the last. She pushed through the underbrush, branches scraping her skin. Then she heard it. A soft whine, low and strained.

Twenty feet ahead, barely visible in the cloud covered moonlight, Max stood with his head low, paws scratching desperately at the ground. Joan stilled herself, using the shotgun to steady her trembling hands as she took a cautious step forward. She swallowed, watching her loyal companion, his usually powerful stance replaced by a strange urgency.

Max whined again, glancing at her with desperate eyes before resuming his digging.

In the darkness, it took her a moment to realize what she was seeing. The pale sliver of a small hand peeked through the freshly disturbed dirt. She froze, heart pounding as a rush of memories flooded her; the laughter Joan seldom heard, Carrie's wide, frightened eyes, and her quiet voice that haunted Joan. For a brief, paralyzing moment, her mind rebelled, refusing to accept what Max had uncovered.

It was Carrie.

Joan's stomach lurched as reality hit with cold, merciless clarity. She dropped to her knees, feeling the grit of the earth press against her as she leaned closer. Glancing around, she saw no sign of Jeb and heard only the soft rise and fall of Max's breathing. Gritting her teeth, she flipped on the flashlight, covering it partially with her hand to keep the glow as dim as possible.

The small body in the shallow grave was battered, almost unrecognizable. Max had uncovered her head and part of her right shoulder, her tiny frame lying in a bed of earth she would never rise from. Bruises darkened her face and neck, swollen beyond recognition. Horror rooted Joan in place, her gaze locked on Carrie's broken form as tears began to sting her eyes.

A raw, consuming rage rose from within her, an emotion so fierce it nearly tore her apart. She clenched her fists until her nails bit into her palms, needing something, anything, to hit, to break. But there was nothing here she could punish, nothing she could tear apart that would make this right. Neither anger nor sorrow could begin to contain the depth of what she felt.

A primal injustice ripped through her, fierce and unrelenting, taking over every rational thought. Her hands shook with an almost feral need to strike back, to make someone, no, Jeb Hogg, suffer for what he'd done.

There was nothing left to think about, nothing more to question. Her body vibrated with a brutal determination, an instinct to avenge every child who had ever been hurt by hands that should have held them gently.

The bitter, blinding hatred left no room for doubt. She felt the clarity, cold and precise, settle in her bones. It was too late for Carrie and her mother. But for Jeb Hogg, she could still serve justice. She would make him pay.

Chapter Seventeen

Deadly Insanity

Joan didn't know how long she'd sat beside Carrie's small, fragile body. She allowed a fog of sorrow to overcome the rage for a short time. Max lay beside her, pressing his warmth against her leg, offering comfort. Her anger built again along with the ache of failure. She couldn't shake the memory of staring straight into Jeb's eyes when he pointed the shotgun at her. She'd had her chance. She could have pulled the trigger, ending his reign of terror. Instead, she'd run, and the shame of it gnawed at her insides.

She brushed the track of tears from her face. Thinking this way wouldn't get the job done. That job was killing Jeb Hogg. He wouldn't just pay for what he'd done to Carrie and Susan, he would pay for Sammy's death, Willow's incarceration, and most of all, Joan's failure to end Todd's life so Willow didn't suffer for it. She shook her head sharply, the ballcap slipping from her head and landing in the dirt, as her grief pivoted into a focused, hot rage. Jeb Hogg would pay, and she would remember Carrie's bruised, fragile face forever. His only chance now was to kill her first.

A prickle ran down the back of her neck. Jeb was coming; she felt it.

"We're going to circle around and head back to the bad place," she murmured to Max, resting a hand on his scruffy head. "Hopefully, it'll throw him off long enough to buy us some time." She set her cap back on, turning it backward, not caring that her white hair stuck out in every direction. Max followed her as she took off in the opposite direction of her property. Two of Jeb's sons were dead, and possibly a third. Her odds of getting help from the remaining son were slim. Still, she had to take the chance.

The ridge ahead was steeper than the others she'd climbed that night. With every step, her body protested, pain tightening in her muscles, especially her calf. She pushed it down, forcing her mind into steely resolve.

Then, a low whine broke the silence. She stilled, her hand reflexively going to Max's collar, calming him as he released a quiet grumble. Out of the darkness, a dog emerged, its body low, tail wagging cautiously. Joan's heart sank. It was one of Jeb's. Faint squeaks and tiny grunts sounded from the bushes.

"Crap," she whispered, crouching low and extending her hand. "Hey there, mama," she cooed softly, her voice gentle and high-pitched.

The dog approached slowly, her tail wagging with hopeful energy, even as her body language suggested she expected a strike. Joan's heart clenched at the sight. The dog sniffed her fingers, ignoring Max, who stood calmly beside Joan. After a tentative sniff, the dog leaned in, allowing Joan to run her hand over her thin fur. The whimpers in the bushes grew louder, and Joan glanced toward them.

From her pocket, she pulled a handful of dog food, letting the mother lick her palm clean in a matter of seconds. "Thirsty?" she asked gently, unscrewing her water bottle and filling its cap. The dog lapped it up gratefully, and Joan refilled it twice more before the animal finally seemed content. "Can I look at your babies?" she asked in a soft murmur.

The dog continued licking at the cap. Joan stepped closer to the bush, parting a few low-hanging branches. She saw them. Four squirming, black-coated puppies, nestled into a small hollow. Max sniffed at the air, his stub tail giving a friendly wiggle. He'd always loved other dogs, thanks to the dog park trips Joan had managed, even if they were rare these days. But Max had learned to socialize young, and he stayed back, letting the mother feel safe.

The puppies looked like perfect little replicas of their mama, with shiny black fur and small, soft bodies, though one had a white spot on its hind leg and backside, a sweet mark of distinction. Joan wondered how the mother had kept them alive, how she'd stayed so gentle and trusting after a life with Jeb. There was something almost heroic about her resilience.

Reaching into her pocket, Joan emptied the rest of the dog food onto the ground. Max didn't protest. He understood that the other dog needed it more than he did.

Joan poured more water for the mother, watching her drink it down with desperate gratitude. The poor dog's sides heaved, her ribs sharp and visible beneath her dark coat, and her swollen teats sagged with milk. Joan estimated the puppies were about three weeks old.

She rubbed the dog's head. Somehow, Joan would find a way to save this mother and her pups. The dog had fought too hard. She could do the same.

It suddenly occurred to Joan; Carrie had to be the reason this mama escaped. Carrie's kindness was instinctual and somehow survived despite the abuse. She'd often told Joan about the wildlife she tried to help. Joan's sadness almost took over again, so she pushed it back with rage.

"If I can, I will come back for you, girl," Joan whispered, her voice barely steady as she poured one last capful of water for the dog. The mother drank eagerly, her tail giving a hopeful wag. Joan lingered, rubbing her hand along the dog's head one more time, as though making a silent promise.

With a final look, she turned to go, leading Max away from the small family. The mother dog followed them for about twenty feet, torn, before turning back to where her puppies waited, releasing a small whine that hung in the air like an unspoken plea.

It took more than thirty grueling minutes to circle around and approach Jeb's property from the main road. By the time she arrived, her legs felt as if they might give out beneath her, but Max leaned in as they walked, his warm weight holding her upright. Without him, she wasn't sure she'd still be on her feet.

She glanced ahead. The fire pit was nearly burned out. This would be the real test.

The barn.

The structure stood ahead of her, newer than the other buildings. Yet, despite the newer construction, the double barn doors looked battered and worn, the wood splintered and hanging loosely from its hinges. The doors radiated neglect, and a sense of foreboding filled Joan. She steeled herself, moving forward. She gave the right-side door a careful push. It creaked loudly, an agonizing sound that made her freeze, her heart pounding.

A chorus of barks erupted from within, loud and frantic, filling the air with wild, fevered energy. Max bristled beside her, his lips pulling back in a low growl.

"No," she whispered, bending down to look him in the eyes. "If you can't be quiet, I'll leave you out here." Her voice was firm, and Max went silent, his gaze steady, as though understanding the gravity of the moment.

No dogs came rushing to investigate, and that only confirmed her suspicions. They were caged, or worse, chained up and unable to move. She took a deep breath, and slipped inside, closing the door behind them.

CHAPTER EIGHTEEN

PUPPY DOG TAILS

THE BARN HAD TO be at least eight hundred square feet, with no windows or even a back door that she could see. Rows of wire cages lined the far wall, stacked two high, the metal bars rusted and bent. Joan stepped forward, forcing herself to ignore the sharp, sickening stench of urine, feces, and the unmistakable tang of decay similar to what she's smelled inside the home. Bile rose in her throat.

On the wall to her right, ten empty cages sat on a wood frame. They had to be for the dogs Jeb left at her place. The real horror was straight ahead. Her flashlight trembled slightly as she shined it from one cage to another, her horror growing with each glance. The dogs on the lower row stood in three to four inches of filth, a sludge-like, greenish, oily mess. It coated their paws and fur. There was no bedding, nothing soft to shield them from the cold floor. These poor animals were left in tiny prisons, existing only to suffer.

She moved the light across their bodies, revealing emaciated frames and jutting ribs. Many had open sores, raw and festering, with patches of fur missing, their exposed skin cracked and irritated. Some eyes were swollen shut from infection, milky with pus. This was where spirits came to die, she thought, looking into their dull, vacant eyes. They growled, some snapped at the air, and others howled.

In one cage, a female dog lay nursing a small litter of pups, her body curled protectively around them. At the beam of Joan's flashlight, she bared her teeth, too tired to even growl. Joan understood. Even in a place like this, the mother was willing to fight for what little she had.

Then her flashlight fell on something worse: a dog, shriveled and dried almost beyond recognition. The small, lifeless form was curled in the corner of its cage, fur matted against shrunken skin. It had been there for weeks, maybe months, rotting in the same filth that surrounded the others. Joan realized the smell of death lingered beneath the other odors.

She drew in a shaky breath, feeling her heart twist painfully in her chest. She pulled the light away, too sickened to see more.

The heat in the barn was stifling, even with the night outside at a much lower temperature. There was no ventilation, just a thick, stagnant warmth that made breathing feel like swallowing sludge. As she walked toward a rusted metal bucket in the corner, a rat scurried out, leaping past her flashlight beam. She jolted back, stumbling as her heart pounded against her ribs.

Turning back toward the rows of cages, her vision blurred with angry tears. There was nothing she could do right now to help them. It gnawed at her, leaving her feeling raw and hollow. She clenched her fists, knowing these animals deserved better.

Joan had to escape the barn. The scale of suffering was like a weight pressing down on her chest, suffocating her. She forced herself to take a deep breath, bracing against the nausea stirred by the putrid air. She made one last sweep of the flashlight over the barn's interior. As she moved the light, something unusual caught her eye, stopping her in her tracks.

She stepped closer, squinting, trying to make sense of what she was seeing. Several stovetops, microwave ovens, and hot plates were crowded onto a counter at the far end of the barn, each one plugged into a tangled mess of cords snaking toward a power strip. Her eyes traced the thick, worn cord running from the strip to a grimy generator in the corner. Her fingers shook as the beam of her flashlight revealed glass bottles, plastic containers, and rows of flasks and tubes crammed along the counter, covering every inch of the stained, cluttered surface.

An old bookcase leaned against the wall beside the counter, lined with cans of acetone, paint thinner, and other substances with faded labels she didn't immediately recognize. Her gaze lingered on one small bottle labeled "red phosphorus," and beside it, a cardboard box stuffed with bubble packets of small, red pills. She moved the flashlight over the rest of the shelf, seeing more chemicals—Drano, bleach, and a large bucket scrawled with the words "anhydrous ammonia" in black marker.

The realization hit her like a punch to the gut. She was standing in a meth lab. The dogs were being raised here, breathing in the poisonous fumes, enduring it as part of their horrid lives. She swallowed hard, resisting the urge to bolt. Every instinct screamed that she and Max needed to get out of there before they inhaled any more of the toxic air.

With clenched fists, she muttered a string of curses directed at the sheriff's department, frustration and anger rising. If they had listened to her, if they'd bothered to investigate this place, if they'd just taken the time to interview Carrie or her mother, maybe they would have discovered the horrors hidden in this barn. So much suffering could have been prevented if anyone had cared to look a little closer.

And yet, a small, unexpected thought pierced through the chaos in her mind: none of the dogs here showed signs of rabies. The possibility of a silver lining crossed her mind. If these poor animals weren't infected, then maybe there was some hope after all, a chance that she could help them, however small that chance felt.

It took everything she had to turn away, to step back toward the door. She felt as if the animals' eyes were on her, watching her leave, their silent pleas haunting her as she tried to reassure them with the same promise she'd made to the mother dog. "I promise I'll do everything I can to save you," she whispered, her voice thick with emotion. She took a last look, hoping they understood, even though she wasn't sure she could keep her word.

Regardless of what happened to her, law enforcement would eventually be forced to inspect this property. Deputy Berger, at least, would discover the truth.

She stepped outside and froze.

Fire.

Flames danced wildly from the house, orange and red tongues licking up toward the sky, casting flickering shadows across the property. Smoke billowed out, thick and dark, swallowing the stars overhead. Sick dread clenched inside her. Jeb was back, and he'd set his own place on fire. She reached out for Max, but he'd already bolted, his dark shape disappearing into the chaos.

Joan instinctively slipped her flashlight into her pocket, leaving her hands free to grip the shotgun. Her pulse hammered as she crouched low, melting into the shadows, her eyes darting for cover. The nearest decrepit vehicle, a rusting sedan resting in the dirt, offered a small refuge. She ducked behind it, peering around just in time to hear Max's bark, sharp and challenging. A low growl from another dog followed, echoing across the yard just before a violent clash erupted. Max had run into Jeb's beast.

She stepped out from behind the car, muscles coiled to sprint to the next cover, when a deafening roar filled her ears. She turned just as Jeb's truck surged forward, barreling toward her. His eyes gleamed wild and unhinged through the windshield, an expression twisted with pure insanity as he floored the gas, speeding straight at her. There was barely a moment to react. She dove beneath the car just as his truck crashed into it, the impact sending her against the far tire. Pain lanced up her side.

Gears screeched as Jeb yanked the truck into reverse, grinding it into gear to try to hit the vehicle again. Adrenaline flooded her veins as she rolled away from the tire. There was nowhere else to go. She tried to wriggle out from the opposite side, but Jeb rammed the truck forward again, metal shrieking as the vehicle shuddered under the force. She grabbed onto the undercarriage, feeling the raw edge of steel dig into her fingers as she let it drag her a few feet. The truck finally ground to a halt, and she took her chance, rolling quickly out from the opposite side.

Gasping, she looked up to see the house engulfed, flames leaping from every window and moving dangerously toward the barn. Her stomach twisted as she imagined the animals inside. If the fire reached the barn, the chemicals would explode. The thought offered only a hollow irony—death by explosion would be a mercy compared to the life they'd led. Unfortunately, mercy had never found a way onto this property.

Tires squealed as Jeb maneuvered the truck looking for a target. Joan darted toward the house, circling around the side to avoid his line of sight. As she rounded the corner to the backyard, she froze again.

Max was down, the brindle pinning him to the ground. Her rottweiler's chest heaved as he tried to shake the larger dog off, but the brindle's jaws were clamped around his throat, its powerful body keeping Max pinned. Joan's mind raced as she realized her shotgun was gone and somewhere in the wreckage from Jeb's assault. She sprinted toward the dogs, hand going for her handgun in its holster. The truck's engine roared behind her, the headlights sweeping across the yard as Jeb hunted her.

"Max!" she screamed, the word torn from her throat.

With a desperate surge, Max managed to get his feet under him, the brindle's jaws still fastened around his throat. He shook furiously, his collar offering little protection, and he was running out of strength. She sprinted forward, gun in hand. Max broke free and bolted toward her, his eyes wild. The brindle ran off.

She glimpsed a shed about twenty yards away, the only possible cover. If she went inside, Jeb would likely crash the truck into it.

"Come on, Max!" she hissed, taking off toward the shed's back corner. They reached it just as Jeb's truck skidded to a stop, the headlights blazing, casting stark shadows across the yard. She pressed herself and Max tight against the outer shed wall. The truck's rumble faded while she looked around wildly for a place to go.

The engine cut off. The only sound was the loud crackling of the house fire.

For a heartbeat, she and Max stood in the suffocating silence, her hand clenched tightly around the gun as she strained to hear. She held her breath, every nerve on edge. Jeb was out there with the brindle, somewhere in the dark.

CHAPTER NINETEEN

DESTRUCTIVE CHAOS

J OAN SCANNED THE DARK for the brindle, but it was nowhere in sight. Relief mixed with urgency as she spotted a thick, shaggy-bark tree about twenty feet away, its trunk wide enough to offer decent cover. Several dense bushes flanked it, creating a small haven.

"Max, hurry," she whispered, nudging him forward as she made a dash for it. She slipped behind the tree, positioning Max in the small space at her side, her handgun at the ready, wishing she still had the shotgun. Her grip tightened, prepared to fire if she got the chance.

The flames from the house reached higher, their heat grating on her skin even from a distance. She cast a desperate glance toward the barn, knowing the animals trapped inside didn't have much time before the fire reached them. Another sound interrupted her thoughts: a sharp, piercing whistle, drifting through the night from farther away than she'd expected Jeb to be.

A cold chill raced down her spine. Was it one of his sons? She hadn't noticed the body from the dog attack lying in the yard, and if that son survived, she was now up against not just Jeb but possibly two more Hoggs. Any hope she had that the boys would help disappeared after she found the meth lab.

Joan calmed herself with deep, steady breaths so she could think. If she could reach the barn and open the cages, she could add to the chaos. Her rage had grown to something indescribable. She wasn't going down without a fight, and she would not give up. Carrie and Susan were dead, and this was now retribution.

A shotgun blast startled her so badly she flinched. The boom was followed by a rapid volley of pops. Jeb's ammunition was exploding inside the burning house. She crouched lower, her arm instinctively wrapping around Max, who leaned against her, tense but silent. The sporadic bursts continued, and she took another steady breath, tightening her other hand on the gun. There would be no running this time.

She glanced at Max, and her heart clenched. A three-inch flap of skin hung open on his left shoulder, blood matting the fur around it. The brindle would kill him in another fight. She searched desperately for a better place to hide. The realization was settling in that neither she nor Max would get out of this alive. She wouldn't let that stop her, but her heart cried for her friend who had done nothing but give her love.

An eight-foot ridge rose up thirty feet away, its incline steep but not impossible. If they could make it over, they'd reach the dirt road on the other side. The road went east toward St. Johns, a small town with little charm but one critical feature: the sheriff's department. Unfortunately, the road had little cover, and she doubted her leg would hold for a fifteen-mile walk. She would be a sitting duck for Jeb.

The only chance she had was to do the unexpected. She had to strike first before Jeb or his sons had the chance. Jeb might be rabid, but she was prepared to match his insanity with her own.

She waited for the right moment. Roaring flames filled the air, drowning out every other noise. Now.

She met Max's steady gaze, and he stared back, unblinking. "We're going after him," she said, her voice barely audible above the inferno. Max's ears perked up, and he slowly blinked in acknowledgment. Not a whimper or bark escaped him. He was ready. "You need to pull me up that ridge," she whispered, tightening her grip on his collar.

"Heel," she instructed softly, and together, they began the slow, grueling climb up the mound of dirt and rock. With every step, pain shot through her injured leg, her joints grinding with each weight shift. She gritted her teeth and pushed on. Max climbed steadily, offering her just enough support to keep going. The hill felt endless. She could almost feel a hot gun barrel pressed against her back, ready to fire.

They reached the top, and Joan's balance wavered as she took her first step down the other side, her legs ready to give out. She lowered herself carefully to the ground, dropping beside Max, both of them breathing heavily. They didn't have time to rest, but her body refused to go on without a break. Reaching into her pocket, she pulled out the last of her water. She took a small sip to wash the grime from her mouth, then poured the rest into the cap, holding it out for Max. He drank it all, licking the plastic clean before looking back up at her.

After gaining her feet, she took a few cautious steps downward, keeping her body low, braced to duck if needed. Once her head was low enough to stay below the ridge, she straightened up and surveyed the area. The height of the hill tapered down at the ridge's edge. She'd have a clear view of the driveway if she went there.

The fire blazed, casting an eerie glow from above and making her nerves prickle. The small town's volunteer fire department wouldn't be arriving any time soon. Friday nights meant everyone was at the football game, including the volunteers.

By the time anyone got here, the barn and everything inside would be lost.

For some reason, the memory of Deputy Berger's offhanded advice came back to her. It was after she'd purchased the shotgun. *"If you aim that thing, shoot to kill."* She'd shrugged it off, but tonight, that piece of advice was her goal. She intended to follow it to the letter.

She made her way to the edge of the ridge and gestured for Max to sit. She took two careful steps forward, peering around a cluster of rocks. Her heart thumped. Jeb's truck remained parked in front of the shed. There was no sign of him in the driver's seat or in the corner of the yard she could see.

She took a cautious step into the open.

The blast came out of nowhere.

She was flung to the right as the buckshot tore into her left side, the impact like a wall of needles ripping through her. Pain exploded down her ribs, her shoulder, her thigh. She hit the ground hard, gasping. Her vision blurred. A dark, sick feeling swept over her. She barely made out Jeb's shout above the ringing in her ears.

"Get him!" he yelled.

The brindle.

She didn't need to see to know the dog was coming. Her gun had slipped from her hand when she fell, and she scrambled frantically in the dirt, fingers clawing at the ground until she felt the cold grip.

The brindle didn't charge around the ridge as she'd expected.

Max's body went rigid, his gaze snapping upward. Joan followed his line of sight.

The brindle stood above them on the ridge, framed in the glow of the fire like some demonic creature. He loomed, a hulking figure of muscle and fury, his lips peeled back in a grotesque snarl that showed every jagged, yellowed tooth in his mouth. Thick strands of foamy saliva hung from his jaws, dripping slowly to the dirt below. His amber eyes were feral, lit by a terrifying, unrestrained rage that zeroed in on her with pure, violent hunger. The deep growl that rolled from his throat vibrated through the ground beneath her.

He leapt.

CHAPTER TWENTY

UNSTOPPABLE HAVOC

H ER BODY MOVED ON instinct, the gun coming up in her hands as she braced herself.

Max launched himself between her and the brindle, dislodging the gun from her hand before she fired. The two dogs became a blur of snapping teeth and thrashing bodies a few feet away.

Max's high-pitched yelp sliced through the air, freezing Joan's blood. Ignoring the sharp pain radiating through her side and leg, she scrambled to her knees and searched for the gun. Her fingers found it, her grip tightening as she brought it to her chest.

She sighted down the barrel. The dogs rolled, and she couldn't take the shot without risking Max. She cursed under her breath, her hands trembling from adrenaline and terror. Jeb had to be close.

The seconds dragged. The brindle tore more flesh from Max's shoulder, and her beautiful dog, so full of heart, fell, his cry ringing in her ears. Helpless anger churned inside her, but her hands wouldn't stop shaking. She was dying inside, her fear a poison spreading through her. Curling the fingers of her left hand into the ground, she let jagged stones dig into her palm and beneath her nails as she waited for a shot.

The growls and cries stopped, their fight moving into the shadows.

The pull on her heart was almost too much. She didn't think it was Max who had survived. She rolled onto her back, staring at the smoky night sky. This was how it ended.

Her eyes fell to the gun in her right hand. Her entire body shook. She rolled partially to her side and forced herself to glance away from Max's shadow.

Jeb was back in his truck, the driver's side door flung open. His face twisted with rage as he slapped the dashboard, the truck's engine whining and sputtering. The gears ground noisily as he jerked the stick, either unable to get it into gear or completely forgetting the clutch. His movements were erratic, his mind unraveling right before her eyes. He was still dangerous, still deadly, and worst of all, he would win this battle.

A warm, wet tongue touched the back of her neck. She exhaled the breath she'd been holding.

"Max."

She turned, and there he was, his muzzle bloodied but his eyes steady and loyal as he settled beside her. A few feet away, the brindle dragged itself closer before collapsing, twitching in the dirt. Its head lifted once, but then it slumped back and went still.

A strange mix of relief and sadness tightened in her chest. Even though Max had taken out the brindle, she felt herself giving in to death. Blood seeped into the dirt from so many small wounds. Max would never meet Willow. She pulled him close, and he licked her face this time, letting out a soft whine.

The sound conveyed so much. Joan realized she was letting pain and fear rule her again. She wasn't a quitter. The worst that could happen was death, and she had only one choice: keep going.

"We've got to end this," she whispered, her voice thick with pain, as she looked into Max's weary eyes.

Max let out another soft, distressed whine, his body trembling with exhaustion too.

"Come on," she insisted, but he didn't rise. She slowly backtracked ten feet in case Jeb waited at the driveway to shoot her again if she came around the ridge. Each step hurt but only gave her more resolve. They had to somehow make it back over the ridge. "Up," she commanded in her no-nonsense training voice when she thought she'd made it far enough.

Max struggled to his feet, his movements slow and labored. Joan gathered herself for the climb when he made it to her side. Her legs felt like lead, every muscle burning with fatigue, but she gritted her teeth, refusing to let Jeb win. Glancing down at her torn, bloodied side, she forced herself to stand fully upright. Each step sent fresh waves of agony through her body.

"We can do this," she rasped, her voice little more than a whisper, as they took one step, then another.

Max practically pulled her along. She didn't look up, down, or back. Each step was wrenched from her by sheer force of will. Her grip on Max slipped as a dizzy spell overtook her, and she landed face-first on the ground.

For a moment, she lay there, dirt and grit clinging to her face. Then she stretched out a hand, grasping at sparse grass and using it to drag herself up an inch, then another. Finally, she raised her head, sucking in a breath as the ridge's peak came into view just a few feet away. A little more. She was so close.

At the top, she could make out Jeb, who had just leapt out of the truck. His figure blurred until she blinked, forcing her vision to steady. He spun in a slow, furious circle, cursing loudly. Was he looking for the brindle? He froze, staring down the driveway before breaking into a full run.

She rolled over to the house side of the ridge. Her vision blurred, and she fought down nausea that surged with every wave of dizziness. Placing a hand on her side, she felt her shirt completely soaked in blood. After a few deep breaths, she tried to stand, but her legs buckled, sending her tumbling down the incline.

A stubborn shrub stopped her fall, jarring her painfully. Dark agony consumed her. A throbbing, indistinguishable ache that blurred the lines of her injuries. She no longer knew where one wound ended, and another began.

Max's tongue swiped across her face, snapping her out of the haze. He stood over her, his steady licks keeping her grounded, pulling her back from the mental darkness.

"One more time," she whispered in determination. Slowly, she forced herself to stand, swaying as pain radiated through her. She kept her gaze fixed on the far side of the house, her only chance to stay out of Jeb's line of sight. She stumbled forward, focusing her mind on the movement, forcing the pain to separate from the reality of her nightmare.

The house fire had dwindled, but as she moved, she saw new flames shoot up, brighter and farther away. Her heart sank. The barn was burning now. She couldn't let the dogs die like that.

Finally, she reached the barn doors, leaning heavily against them to stay upright as she pushed both sides fully open. Smoke hung inside, stinging her eyes and throat. Flames licked the loft area closest to the house. The dogs howled and barked in terror.

"Come on, Max," she urged, leaning on him for support as they stumbled deeper inside.

She freed dog after dog, her hands working on autopilot even as dizziness threatened to knock her down. The mother dog bolted with a pup in her jaws, fleeing toward freedom. Each unlatched door was a small victory against the rising flames.

The heat grew unbearable, creeping up her spine as the fire spread. Smoke thickened, choking her, and tears streamed down her soot-streaked face.

The next cage held no sound. Through the haze, she saw the dog inside; still and unmoving. The one above it was the same, poisoned by the air near the meth lab. The mother dog came back for another puppy.

Joan's chest tightened. She and Max had to get out before the building erupted.

Stumbling toward the exit, she fell and finally rolled until she was free, fresh air flooding her lungs.

Max limped over, his soft whine grounding her as she pulled herself to her knees.

Her gaze locked on Jeb's truck. She crawled to it, ignoring the growls echoing nearby. The door handle was warm in her grasp. It opened easily.

"Up," she commanded hoarsely. Max leapt inside, and she clambered in after him, shielding him with her body.

The keys dangled from the ignition.

The explosion rocked the truck, reverberating through the metal as the windshield cracked under the blast. Joan turned her head to the fractured glass and froze.

Jeb stood outside, his face blackened, his eyes blazing with unhinged madness.

Chapter Twenty-One

Absolute Reckoning

JEB RAISED THE SHOTGUN, his face void of emotion, his entire being focused on killing her. There was no sneer, no twisted grin, just a grim, single-minded blaze in his eyes.

Joan bent over Max, shielding him with her body, knowing it wouldn't stop what was coming, but it was all she had. Her heartbeat thundered in her ears as she braced for the blast.

A scream tore through the night, filled with agony so raw it clawed at her eardrums. It took a moment for Joan to realize it hadn't come from her. Jeb's voice, hoarse and guttural, pierced the truck's interior. The sound of his pain reverberated deep within her, but to Joan, it was the sweetest sound she'd ever heard.

She forced herself up, clutching the dashboard with trembling fingers, and looked out. The dogs she'd freed from the cages had pulled Jeb down. They tore at him, a frenzy of snarls, snapping teeth, and flashing fur. His shotgun fell to the ground, and he kicked wildly, trying to fight them off. His screams grew louder, the shrill pitch laced with panic and desperation.

It didn't last long enough. Time blurred, and the world dimmed around her.

Max lay still beneath her, his body unmoving. Joan felt a faint smile creep onto her lips as she rested her weight on him. "We did it," she murmured, her voice barely audible.

Max quivered. A small, slight movement. She didn't know if it was exhaustion or the slow grip of death.

"Stay with me," she whispered, her throat raw from smoke and effort.

Flashing red and blue lights broke through the haze, their piercing glow illuminating the truck's cab. Joan squinted as the colors danced across the windshield, almost too bright to bear. A rifle cracked in the distance, then another. Shouts followed as men, likely sheriff's deputies, approached.

She released a shallow breath, her body sagging. Blood soaked her side and pant leg, warm and sticky. She didn't know if Max would survive his injuries, but she knew one thing for certain: Jeb Hogg was dead.

With every ounce of strength she had left, she pushed herself up halfway, slumping against the door. Her vision flickered, fading in and out. The passenger door creaked open, and Deputy Berger's voice, thick with concern, cut through her fog.

"Joan?"

"Don't let Max out," she groaned, barely able to force the words out.

Berger shifted into the cab. "Move over, you big bear," he muttered gently to Max, his tone betraying an unusual softness. He turned his head and shouted back to his team, "She's in here!" His arm stretched across Max to clasp Joan's hand.

The radio crackled and Berger spoke into it, "Get medical over here immediately."

"How bad are you hurt?" he asked, his voice low and steady.

No time for stupid questions. Each word was a struggle as she rasped, "I... moved the lockbox to the root cellar. Everything Willow needs... it's there."

She wasn't sure if she'd spoken aloud or if the words had only echoed in her mind. Her breaths came in shallow gasps, but she pushed herself to keep going. "Take care of Max until Willow comes home. Jeb had rabies. Quarantine Max, don't let them put him down."

Her thoughts swirled, a tangled mess, her brain sifting through what Berger needed to know. "Carrie's body is out there," she whispered, struggling for air. She tried to point, but her arm was too heavy to lift. "Susan... dead in the house. Don't... forget the rabies... the momma dog and her puppies... near Carrie."

"Joan, you're going to be okay," Berger assured, but his voice wavered.

Stupid man. Her hand tightened on his with surprising force, and she locked eyes with him. "Promise me you'll take care of Max and Willow, you old windbag." Her voice cracked and faltered.

"You know I will. Stop talking like that. Just tell me; what are your injuries?"

Her vision blurred, the edges of her world turning black. His voice sounded farther and farther away. He hadn't said it. He hadn't promised. She clung to the last remnants of her strength.

"Promise," she whispered, her tone fierce despite its weakness.

"Promise," he replied, his voice barely above a whisper, but it was enough.

Relief washed over her as her grip loosened. Her fingers trembled as she laid her palm on Max's back. She felt the faint rise and fall of his chest.

Her lips brushed his ear as she bent close. Her voice was a soft, final murmur, carrying all the love and desperation she felt. "Live for me, Max. Take care of Willow."

Chapter Twenty-Two

Prison Bars

Two weeks later...

THE DRIVE TO PRISON didn't take long enough for Dale Berger. He wasn't ready to face Willow, to deliver the weight of the news he carried. He had rehearsed the words, discarded them, and finally came to accept there was nothing he could say to soften what he came to tell her.

Not long after Joan had moved onto her property, Dale had taken it upon himself to find out more about her. He'd looked her up online, curiosity leading him to the quiet secret of Willow, the granddaughter Joan only spoke about once. She'd casually mentioned Willow and the strongbox. "If anything happens," she'd said, though she never shared more. Dale had laughed it off at the time, joking that Joan would likely outlive him, never knowing how much those words would weigh on him now.

The day before, he had called the prison to arrange this meeting. Given the circumstances, the staff had been accommodating, though they told him Willow wouldn't be permitted to attend the funeral. Not that Joan had wanted one. She'd made it clear in the letter Dale now carried in his jacket pocket, carefully folded and pressed against his chest.

He flashed his badge at the front, explained his purpose, and was quickly escorted to a private visitation room. He wore plain clothes, hoping to avoid overwhelming Willow with the uniformed presence of law enforcement. He sat at the table, his nerves twisted as he waited for her.

When the door opened, she entered with a cautious expression, looking at him inquisitively. Dale rose.

"I'm Dale Berger," he introduced quietly watching the understanding dawn in her eyes.

Her expression shattered, a flicker of dread replacing the quiet expectation. Her head moved in a slow, resisting shake.

"Sit down, please," he urged, his tone almost pleading.

"She's dead, isn't she?" Willow's voice broke.

"Please, sit down," he repeated, gently, coaxing her.

She didn't sit. Instead, she sank to the floor, her gaze locked onto his as her hands went to her hair, clutching it as if it could keep her grounded.

"Don't... don't do this," she begged.

Dale crouched beside her, keeping his voice steady. "I have a letter from your grandmother," he said. "She was the bravest person I've ever known. Please, Willow, come sit and let me explain."

After a moment, he helped her to her feet and guided her to a chair. Pulling his chair close. He took her trembling hand in his, surprised when she didn't pull away. Her fingers quivered, her lashes fluttered as she fought to hold back tears, and he knew she'd endured far more than her share of hardship. He'd read her court transcripts and knew how the system had failed her.

"I'm Dale Berger," he said again, softer this time, hoping to build some bridge of familiarity.

"The deputy?" Her voice carried a faint, brittle edge.

It hadn't occurred to him she would know who he was. "Yes, the deputy."

"How did she die?" she whispered, her eyes locked on his.

He saw the first glimmer of grief, raw and unprocessed, a wound so deep it hadn't fully settled into pain yet. It lingered in her expression, hanging between disbelief and the first sharp sting of loss. His own grief intensified as he prepared to give her the truth she needed, even if it hurt.

"Did she tell you about the Hoggs?" he asked, testing how much she knew.

"Jeb Hogg." Her tone was almost lifeless, but he could hear the fury simmering beneath it, her gaze hardened as she stared over his shoulder.

"Yes," he replied quietly.

Her eyes shot back to his. "Carrie?"

He shook his head. "It was too late for Carrie. But Joan tried."

Willow's gaze fell to the floor before she lifted it again, hollow but steely. "Tell me."

Dale took a steadying breath and recounted what he knew. It had taken his department a week to figure out the series of events. He told her about the Hoggs destroying Joan's home, her trek through the wilderness, and the relentless search until she found Carrie's body. He spoke about Joan's struggle to survive.

"We couldn't use the bloodhounds because their owner wouldn't take the chance with rabies. It took us half a day to find Carrie's body."

Willow stared at the wall for most of his retelling, as her cheeks became wet with silent tears.

"We found everyone except Lance Hogg, Jeb's son. We suspect he didn't survive long out there. Wildlife likely took care of the body." He paused, letting her absorb what happened. "We're monitoring for rabies in the area now."

The silence between them grew thick. Finally, he broke it, his voice soft but determined. "Willow, I want to help."

She shook her head.

"Don't refuse when you haven't heard what I'm offering yet," he said gently. "I loved your grandmother. I never told her, because she was an ornery old bird, but I loved her. And, I know she loved you. I want to honor her by helping you." Willow looked at him. "My place isn't much; I live in a travel trailer about five miles from your grandmother's property. I'm retiring from the sheriff's department, so I'll have plenty of time to do what needs doing." Her expression didn't change. "If Joan's property is not kept up, it won't be worth living in by the time you get out. My offer is this: I'll move my trailer there and repair the damage. I'll keep the place livable, and it won't get ransacked." He rushed the next part. "I'll visit here monthly like she did, if you'll have me as a friend."

Willow studied him for a long, intense moment, her eyes taking him in. "Where is Max?" she asked finally.

"I have him back at my trailer. He's your dog now, but taking care of him is part of my offer," he said firmly. "When you get out, I'll pick you up, move my things off the property, and leave Max with you. I'm happy to put it all in writing so it's official."

A slow nod was her only reply, but her eyes, so similar to Joan's, flickered with a glimmer of hope.

Then her composure crumbled, the weight of grief finally overtaking her as she fell against him. He wrapped his arms around her, holding her tightly as sobs wracked her body. He fought back his own tears, sharing in her loss, giving her a space to mourn, bound by a love for the ornery, fiercely brave woman they'd each lost.

CHAPTER TWENTY-THREE

NEW BEGINNINGS

Seventeen months later...

DALE STOOD OUTSIDE HIS truck, shifting anxiously from foot to foot, his hands tucked into the pockets of his jeans. The Arizona sun was merciless, even in early spring, and despite the air conditioning running inside the truck, he felt the heat pressing down on him. He wasn't sure if his nerves came from anticipation or something deeper, but he suspected Willow felt the same.

Over the past months, they'd grown familiar through his visits. He hadn't known what to expect at first. Joan's absence had left a hollow space in both of their lives, but slowly, cautiously, they had begun to fill it with shared stories and plans for the future. His connection to Willow had deepened as he told her about the repairs he was making to Joan's property, each one a labor of love and grief.

At first, Willow hadn't said much when he spoke about Joan, but she listened intently. Her attention sharpened whenever he mentioned the property—what still needed fixing, the tools he'd borrowed, the things he couldn't quite figure out.

She'd scolded him for using his own money, but he always shrugged it off. "Joan left you enough to get by," he'd insist. "You'll need that money. The work's for me anyway." It was true. Every repair gave him purpose and eased his aching heart.

Now, with her release, his projects were at an end. There'd be no more "just one more repair" to keep him lingering on the property. His focus shifted entirely to Willow's next steps.

He scanned the building for any sign of her, his heart thudding in his chest. When she finally stepped out, dressed in jeans and a simple T-shirt, casual clothes he'd brought her a few weeks ago, he felt an immediate wave of relief.

Her eyes found his, and she smiled faintly. Her steps quickened as she approached, her arms swinging loosely at her sides. Dale stepped forward, meeting her halfway, and without a word, she reached out. He wrapped her in a firm hug, holding her tightly. She clung to him a little longer than he expected, and he gave her a reassuring squeeze before she pulled back. In her right hand, she held a small bundle of papers, likely release documents, and a plastic bag with her personal items.

"I brought a surprise for you," he said, tilting his head toward the truck.

Willow's brows furrowed in curiosity. Peering through the window, she spotted movement. In the backseat cab, two dogs scrambled to press their heads between the seats, tails wagging furiously.

Her eyes widened, and Dale chuckled as he opened the truck door. "Now, remember," he said, addressing the dogs, "be on your best behavior, or no cookies when we get home."

Max leapt out first, landing with a heavy thud. His head swung toward Willow, his tail stub wagging so wildly it blurred. He trotted over to her, his head lowered as he sniffed her from ankles to knees. His tail stilled for a moment, and then he whined, a long, high-pitched sound that broke into a series of whimpers as he pushed his body against her, trembling slightly.

Willow knelt, her hand hovering just above his fur. "Max," she murmured, her voice thick with emotion. His reaction shifted, his sniffing growing frantic, as if he were searching for something familiar in her scent. Recognition flashed in his eyes. He'd found it. The same scent that had clung to Joan after she returned from visiting the prison.

"He knows I'm connected to my grandmother," Willow whispered, her hand finally settling on his head. Max leaned into her touch, his whine softening into a contented grumble.

Daisy waited patiently beside Willow, casting hopeful glances up at her. When Willow turned her attention to the mother dog Dale rescued. Daisy tilted her head and stepped closer, sniffing delicately at her fingers. She was gentler than Max, but no less eager for affection.

"They're both big babies," Dale said with a grin. "You'll get used to them fast. Daisy here is the momma dog I told you about. She's my girl now, and Max is yours. Anytime you need, I'll dog sit."

Willow smiled faintly, her hand moving from Max to Daisy. Both dogs vied for her attention, Daisy nosing her arm while Max gave her fingers an enthusiastic lick.

"You never told me what happened to her puppies," Willow said, looking up at him.

Dale shrugged, his grin widening. "Oh, I found them all good homes. Took a while, but we did it. Daisy wasn't exactly thrilled with me after her vet visit, though. I had her spayed, and she's still a bit salty about it."

He watched as Daisy leaned her head against Willow's thigh, her body relaxing as though sensing she'd found a kindred spirit.

Willow lowered herself to one knee, giggling as both dogs took the opportunity to lavish her with wet, happy kisses. She didn't seem to mind a bit.

"All right, you two, give the poor woman a break," Dale said, pulling the dogs back with a firm tug on their collars. "You'll have hours to get to know her on the drive back."

He turned to Willow, his tone softening. "Now, where to first? Food, the store, anything you need?"

She stood slowly, flinging the dog slobber from her arms as best she could. Dale handed her a white handkerchief which she used to dry the wet remnants. Her smile was small but steady, her eyes bright with something he hadn't seen in a long time.

Hope.

"Just home," she said quietly. "Home sounds perfect."

Dale nodded, opening the passenger door for her. As she climbed in, Max jumped in after her, settling himself protectively at her feet, taking up all the space so she couldn't rest her legs. Dale started to scold the dog, but Willow gently lay her legs and feet across his back and smiled.

Daisy hopped into the back, her tail wagging lazily as she lay down.

Dale started the truck, circled out the way he had entered, and pulled onto the highway. He glanced at Willow. She stared out the window, her hand resting lightly on Max's head, her fingers idly stroking his fur. The small bundle of papers sat forgotten in her lap.

For the first time in months, Dale felt a weight lift from his shoulders. They were headed home.

CHAPTER TWENTY-FOUR

THE CALM

Home

WILLOW STOOD JUST OUTSIDE Dale's truck, staring at her grandmother's legacy. The air was dry, carrying a faint tang of dust and sagebrush. In every direction, the landscape stretched wide and barren, dotted with scruffy shrubs and gnarled trees no taller than ten feet. Farther away, jagged rock formations jutted toward the sky, their muted tones a stark contrast to the pale, cloudless expanse above.

It wasn't what she'd expected, it was more.

Fear and excitement had twisted together inside her for months. After spending most of her life behind bars, the idea of freedom had felt more terrifying than hopeful. Leaving prison without Joan waiting for her had only made it worse. She didn't understand this world, but it was the world her grandmother had fought to give her.

For all its lack of color, the quiet beauty of the land settled deep in her soul.

"I'll hitch my trailer and be out of your hair within the hour," Dale said from behind her. His voice carried a gentleness she'd come to cherish. "I'm sure you need some time to adjust."

He handed her a keyring with at least ten keys dangling from it.

"I'll check in on you each day. There's a cell phone inside, it's yours. My number's plugged in. I'll call, not visit, unless you say it's okay, so don't worry. Joan always grumbled at me for coming uninvited." His face reddened slightly as he added, "She'd ask what I'd do if she was walking around naked. I never caught her, though."

Willow managed a small smile, recognizing his rambling as nervousness. In the months since her grandmother's death, they had become friends. It felt good to have him close, even if she wasn't sure how to say it.

"Will you show me around?" she asked, her voice steadier than she felt.

Dale's face lit up with a grin. "Absolutely."

Max and Daisy bounded out of the truck, sniffing the ground eagerly. Willow's gaze lingered on Max. She'd never had a dog, let alone one so big. His sheer size was intimidating, but his presence brought a strange comfort she hadn't expected.

Dale walked a few feet ahead, speaking over his shoulder. "I'll start with the outside. Then we'll head in."

He led her to the barn, a modest structure with a sturdy rolling door. He had built it with his own two hands and his own money. "This kind of door's easier to secure out here," he said, holding out his hand.

It took Willow a moment to realize he was waiting for the keys. Embarrassed by her hesitation, she fumbled with the ring and handed them over. Dale didn't react to her awkwardness, no impatience, no judgment. He simply unlocked the door and lifted it with ease, passing the keys back to her.

"With someone on the property, there's not much theft," he explained, "but when you leave, you'll need to lock up tight."

Willow followed him inside and froze at the sight of the old Ford truck parked neatly to one side. Its glossy paint gleamed in the dim light, a deep shine that seemed almost alive.

"I spent a lot of time getting her pretty," he said. "There're two sets of keys on the ring," Dale went on, "She's in fine shape. I take her out once a week to keep the battery from dying. They don't make them like this anymore."

"Lucy," Willow whispered, the name catching in her throat.

She stepped closer, her fingers brushing against the cool metal of the door. The flood of emotions was almost too much. She hadn't cried since the day Dale gave her the news about her grandmother's death. Prison had taught her early that tears were a weakness. Vulnerability made you a target.

Now, tears welled in her eyes. She blinked them back, swallowing hard.

"I don't have a driver's license," she said quietly.

"No need to worry about that right now," Dale replied, his tone easy and reassuring. "It's several miles before you hit an incorporated road. You can practice on the flatland around the property. I'll take you out the first time you're ready, or you can figure it out on your own. Your call."

How could she ever explain to him that he wasn't a bother? That he was her lifeline?

"I'll take you to get a license when you're ready," Dale continued. He pointed toward the back of the barn that held an overhead loft. "You could also get a horse. There's a couple living nearby who have some nice ones."

Willow shook her head. "Max is big enough for now," she said, earning a wag of the rottweiler's nubby tail.

Dale chuckled. "Fair enough. One step at a time."

The tour continued at the greenhouse. As soon as they stepped inside, the earthy smell hit her, a clean, vibrant scent of soil and life. Every inch of space was used to grow food.

Hanging vines dripped with tomatoes, and rows of vegetables stretched neatly beneath them.

Willow ran her hand along a nearby leaf, marveling at its texture. The shades of green were overwhelming, vivid and full of promise.

"This will get you through a long winter," Dale said, his voice cutting through her thoughts. "I'll help you keep it going until you're comfortable on your own."

Willow nodded, too overwhelmed to respond.

"Joan would have haunted me if I let the garden die," Dale added with a grin. "She loved this place. Even kept bowls of water out for the mice so they wouldn't nibble on her crops."

Willow smiled for the first time since stepping onto the property.

"She never talked about being one of those vegan folks," Dale continued, "but I didn't find any meat, not even in cans, when I cleaned up. She had a thing for all animals, big or small."

"Thank you," Willow said, though the words felt inadequate.

"Don't thank me yet," Dale replied, his tone light. "You'll pay me back in food. I never knew how good homegrown vegetables could taste. Never imagined I'd take up gardening, but here I am. I should build myself a greenhouse one of these days."

Willow watched as he moved toward the exit. For the first time, she felt a small flicker of belonging.

"Ready for the next leg of the tour?" Dale asked, holding the door open for her.

She nodded, glancing around one last time before stepping outside.

Chapter Twenty-Five

Home and Not Alone

WILLOW STOOD AT THE threshold of her grandmother's home, the keys trembling in her hand. Dale waited patiently beside her, his expression calm but watchful.

"It's just a door," she whispered to herself, drawing in a slow, steadying breath.

She inserted the key into the lock and turned it. The security screen creaked open first, followed by the heavy wooden door, revealing the cool interior. Joan's scent lingered faintly in the air, a mix of woodsmoke, dried herbs, and something uniquely her.

Willow stepped inside.

The front room was simple but inviting, with well-worn furniture that spoke of years of use. A crocheted blanket draped over the back of the couch, its colors faded but still vibrant enough to catch the eye. Bookshelves lined one wall, crammed with a mix of paperbacks and binders labeled with meticulous handwriting.

"The solar batteries and well room are in the back, to the right," Dale said, his voice low so as not to disrupt her moment.

"There's a box fan in there to vent the air, but you'll want to keep the door closed. Battery fumes aren't exactly good for you."

Willow nodded absently, her gaze scanning every detail. She stopped at a small calendar pinned to the refrigerator.

"Your grandmother kept track of everything on that," Dale said, stepping up beside her. "Water filter changes, oil for the generator, firewood deliveries—you name it. She even wrote down the number for the well repair guy, though I doubt she liked him much."

Willow touched the corner of the calendar, her fingers lingering on the thick paper. Each date felt like a whisper from her grandmother, a reminder of the rhythm she had carved out in this remote world.

"She built the inside walls herself," Dale continued, motioning to the wooden beams that gave the house its rustic charm. "Did a damn fine job, though I doubt it would pass a building inspection. People live differently out here. What matters is it's sturdy and comfortable."

Willow's throat tightened as she noticed the imperfections, the slight unevenness of the wall trim, and the sections that were wood and hadn't been painted. Each flaw felt like a fingerprint, a tangible mark of her grandmother's presence.

"This place isn't insured," Dale added, almost as an afterthought. "Not the structure, anyway. Joan set up a policy to cover what's inside, though. Said if it burned down, she'd just live in her truck."

Willow let out a soft, breathy laugh. "That sounds like her."

Dale's expression softened, his gaze drifting over the room. "She loved this place. Fought hard to make it hers."

Willow swallowed against the lump forming in her throat. She could feel her grandmother here, in every corner, every detail.

"The fuse box and inverter are in the well room," Dale said, breaking the silence. "I'll give you a rundown on how it all works. It's a lot to take in, but you'll get the hang of it soon enough."

They moved through the small house, Dale explaining the practical details with patience. He showed her how to operate the ceiling fan, the kitchen lights, and the outdoor floodlights. Each switch felt foreign beneath her fingers, a reminder of how long it had been since she'd controlled anything in her environment.

"Do what you can at your own pace," Dale said gently. "No one's rushing you."

Willow nodded, her chest tightening. She wanted to tell him how much his support meant, but the words caught in her throat.

They entered the bedroom next. It was larger than she expected, twice the size of her prison cell, with a single bed neatly made in the corner. Sunlight streamed through the window, casting a warm glow on the wooden floor.

For a moment, she couldn't breathe. This was hers. Her very own space.

She walked to the window and ran her fingers over the latch. The grate outside was sturdy but designed to swing open from the inside. She unlatched it and pushed it open, letting the sunlight flood in.

Turning to face Dale, she said quietly, "I don't know if I can do this."

Dale stepped closer, his expression calm. "You don't have to do it alone," he said. "I'll help with whatever you need, for as long as you need."

His words brought a flicker of comfort, but the panic still bubbled beneath the surface.

"I'll get my trailer hooked up and head out," Dale said, stepping back to give her space. "Do you have any questions before I go?"

Willow stared at him, her heart pounding. It wasn't the size of the property or the complexity of the utilities that scared her. It was freedom. After so many years of being told when to wake, when to eat, when to sleep, the idea of making her own decisions felt paralyzing.

"Could you stay here tonight?" she asked, her voice trembling.

Dale paused, then nodded. "Of course."

He walked to the front room, picked up the cell phone he'd left on the table, and handed it to her. "This is yours now. No passcode yet, but it's easy to use. Even I figured it out." He winked, his easy grin breaking through the tension.

Willow took the phone.

"I'll make us dinner," Dale said. "We can eat outside while the weather's nice. How does that sound?"

Willow let out a shaky breath and nodded.

"It sounds perfect."

Chapter Twenty-Six

The Nightmare

CONCRETE WALLS, HARSH GRAY, pressed in, suffocating her with their cold, unyielding weight. The narrow halls stretched endlessly, folding tighter with every step. She ran, her chest heaving, her lungs burning. The thin, dry air felt like breathing through cloth, each gasp scratching her throat raw.

A sharp clang of metal doors echoed behind her. Too loud, too close.

They were coming.

She stumbled forward, bare feet pounding against the icy floor. Her soles stung with each step, the sensation grounding her desperation. She had to keep moving. If she stopped, they would catch her.

Her breath came in shallow gasps, panic clawing at her chest. She reached out, grasping for invisible purchase to propel herself forward.

They would find her.

They would drag her back.

She couldn't go back.

The corridor twisted ahead, folding in on itself like a tunnel collapsing under its own weight. She turned sharply and slammed into a wall.

No, not a wall. Blue.

It was him.

A guard in a blue uniform loomed over her, his face massive and distorted, too close to escape. His grin split wide, rows of sharp, gleaming teeth stretching unnaturally.

Her scream tore through her throat, raw and primal.

Willow's eyes flew open. Her heart slammed in her chest, an irregular drumbeat of fear.

She wasn't in her cell.

She gulped in air, her chest heaving as reality crept back in, smoothing the jagged edges of the nightmare. Her fists bunched the quilt in her lap, and she realized she was sitting upright in her grandmother's bed.

It was a dream.

She exhaled slowly, forcing her breath to even out.

The nightmares had haunted her for years. Thoughts of her grandmother had been her only solace in prison, her lifeline in the darkest hours. After Joan passed, her fragile refuge turned to thoughts of Dale, this property, and Max.

She was here now.

To push the nightmare further away, she latched onto the good memories she was making. Maybe someday, the past would stop haunting her.

Dale had made dinner the night before while she worked on a salad with fresh ingredients from the garden. The memory of the smoky grilled chicken made her mouth water.

They'd chatted as they worked, Dale's voice steady and warm as he spoke about the greenhouse, the barn, and everything in between. She'd sensed his loneliness seeping into his words, a yearning for connection that echoed her own.

"Would you like a glass of wine?" he'd asked.

Wine.

Willow had never tried it before. A former cellmate had once brewed some from stolen juice in prison. Several inmates got sick, but she'd only pretended to drink hers, blending in to avoid drawing attention. In prison, standing out wasn't safe.

"I'd like to try a bit," she told Dale, her honesty surprising her.

She rarely pushed the boundaries in prison. Doing so risked more time, and the thought of delaying her release date had terrified her. She had been careful, quiet. Trust no one, she'd learned early on. Her survival had depended on it.

Willow had served her sentence in full. She couldn't vote or own a firearm, but at least no parole officer was breathing down her neck. Parole was the downfall of many inmates, especially those who'd spent most of their lives behind bars. Her sentence had been ten years, three in juvenile and seven in state, with no parole.

She and Dale had talked over dinner, her initial nervousness easing with each sip of wine. The tart, slightly sweet flavor had surprised her, and by the time she finished the glass, she found she liked it. Dale offered her more, but she declined.

"It's different," she said, setting her empty glass down. "I'll have another one tomorrow night."

"Just like Joan," Dale said with a chuckle. "She wasn't much of a drinker. I found a few bottles of wine in the house but nothing stronger."

Willow had loved hearing about her grandmother. Being in her home made it easier to talk about her, and Dale's stories filled in gaps she hadn't known existed.

"I've told you how ornery she was," Dale said with a laugh. "She didn't like me asking personal questions. I learned more about her cleaning up this place than I ever did while she was alive. There's stuff in the closet she left for you. Everything that woman did was with you in mind."

Sadness mixed with love flickered in his eyes.

Willow's chest ached. She understood her grandmother's orneriness now. It came from love and loss.

Joan had been her biggest advocate. Willow had barely known her before the trial, but Joan had sat behind her at every hearing, brushing Willow's shoulder with steady, reassuring fingers whenever she stood. It was the first love Willow had ever truly known.

Her mother had been broken, often reversing their roles so Willow ended up caring for her. When the sentence came down, her grandmother's rage had filled the courtroom. She was escorted out for yelling at the judge.

Her grandmother had been her first champion. Now it was Dale, and Willow realized how odd their situation was—two people tied together by one woman's love.

After dinner, Dale assured her he was only a shout away before heading to his motor home with Daisy in tow, leaving Max behind.

Max followed Willow to the bathroom door, nudging it with his nose as she tried to close it. She laughed, remembering her grandmother telling her how Max had done the same to her.

He waited patiently until she came out, his short tail wagging as if it was the most natural thing in the world.

Willow walked the house, turning on additional lights. Dale had told her to leave the front and back doors open, locking only the security screens to keep the house cool overnight.

She opened her bedroom window and double-checked the latch that secured the grill.

When she finally slipped between the soft covers, she didn't think she'd be able to sleep. But the soothing rhythm of crickets and the faint rustle of the night eased her mind.

Then the dream woke her.

The previous evening's memories calmed her now. She lay back against the sheets, her heartbeat finally normal. Max jumped on the bed and licked her square in the face, making her laugh.

The laughter turned into tears.

She snuggled against Max, wrapping her arms around him as sobs wracked her body. His warm breath fanned her hair, a steady reassurance that she wasn't alone.

In prison, therapy had taught her that crying was healthy, but those women hadn't lived behind bars. They could go home at the end of the day. Crying in prison wasn't good. It made you vulnerable.

Here, she could finally let it out.

Her grandmother's death had left a gaping hole in her heart, sadness a tight fist of grief with no way out. She cried for her grandmother and herself.

Her mother's death lingered like a shadow, stilted memories better left buried. In the juvenile facility, her nightmares had been psychotic recollections of her father. Once transferred to State Prison, the nightmares shifted to her incarceration; guards she didn't trust, women who wanted something from her, and the suffocating isolation.

If not for her grandmother's letters and visits, filling the endless void of hours with love and encouragement, she might not have survived.

Now Dale had stepped into that same space with his calm demeanor and a promise of a place to call her own.

She squeezed Max tightly as the tears slowed. Her stuffed, leaking nose eventually demanded tissues.

She gave Max a gentle push. It did absolutely nothing. He licked her face, and to escape, she rolled in the opposite direction, nearly falling off the bed. Her feet touched the cool tile.

Max jumped down when she walked toward the bathroom.

Before she entered, a sound at the front door made her stop. Daisy waited behind the screen, giving a soft whine.

Willow veered to the door and let Max out before heading to the bathroom.

She glanced at herself in the mirror. The loose nightshirt she wore, a reminder of prison, hung awkwardly on her frame. She hadn't touched her grandmother's closet yet. Willow wanted time to sit and explore her personal belongings.

When she returned to the living room, the sound of barking drew her toward the screen door.

Dale sat on the steps of his travel trailer, his coffee mug in hand, watching the dogs chase each other across the yard. He turned and lifted his cup in greeting.

"Good morning," he said. "Want to join me for coffee?"

"I'll be right out," Willow replied. "Let me get dressed first."

She went back inside, pulling a clean shirt from the bag she'd brought from prison. She slipped into the jeans she'd worn the day before. They were her only pair. She would go through her grandmother's clothes today and see if anything worked.

Eventually, she'd need to go shopping. Having Dale drive her around wasn't ideal. She'd have to learn to drive so she wasn't a burden.

Yesterday had been overwhelming. She'd barely slept the week before her release.

Today, she started with freedom.

Dale handed her a steaming cup of coffee when she joined him outside. "I didn't know if you like it with sugar or black. I have sugar inside if you want to add it."

Willow smiled softly. "Sugar was hit or miss in prison, so I learned to drink it black. I'd like to try one of those fancy coffees someday, though."

She took a cautious sip, and her eyes widened as she met his gaze.

"This is the best coffee I've ever had. I don't think I need anything fancier."

Dale laughed, the lines of his face crinkling. "It's nothing special, but I've had several cups of the swill they serve in jail, and even the dogs wouldn't touch that with a ten-foot pole."

He stood and grabbed a lawn chair leaning against the trailer. "Sit and enjoy. There's more coffee inside. Have you thought about breakfast?"

She shook her head and took another sip. "No, I'm not even sure what's available."

"We can tackle it together. I bought groceries, but I wasn't sure what you liked."

Willow shrugged. "Prison food was like the coffee and usually awful. I have no idea what I like."

"We'll fix that soon enough," Dale said.

His calm presence gave her hope. For the first time in years, she allowed herself to think that there was a lifetime ahead of her.

"I want to learn to cook," she said.

"Joan left you a stack of cookbooks. Once you learn, invite me over and I'll be your first critic. I also wash dishes."

He was teasing her, and she liked it.

"I usually take a short hike in the mornings while the weather is nice," he said. "I found strange footprints down by the wash yesterday and want to check for more. Ranch locals sometimes wander through without realizing they're on private property.

"I also find four-wheeler tracks now and then. It's usually cattlemen checking on livestock. They have free-range out here. There's a watermill that keeps the trough full not far up the road. The cattle walk through the property to get to it."

He laughed. "Joan had a slingshot she used to chase them off. Her ammo of choice was marbles. She threatened me with it once." Laughter filled his voice as he added, "She said the sound scared the cows away, but for me, she'd aim for my head."

He paused, lost in the memory. Willow could see the fondness in his expression, but also the sadness.

Finally, he shook his head. "Those cows like to lean against the solar array, and they can cause damage. If it's not one thing, it's another out here."

He took a sip of coffee, then glanced at her. "What do you say to a short hike?"

Willow hesitated. She wanted to ask him to stay on the property with her and not take his trailer away. It wasn't fair of her to expect him to, and the words caught in her throat. Instead, she smiled and said, "That would be great. Do the dogs get to come?"

"I dare you to leave them behind," Dale replied. "Joan should have some hiking boots in her closet. They'll work until you order your own. Finish your coffee, and we'll head out."

Willow drank the rest of the coffee, savoring the warmth and flavor. When she finished, Dale returned to his trailer, and she stepped inside her grandmother's house.

The scent of cedar and lavender hit her as she opened the closet door. She inhaled deeply, sadness curling tightly in her chest.

This was her grandmother's space.

Tears gathered in her eyes, but she forced them back. Dale was waiting, and curling up on the floor for another cry could wait.

The closet was long, narrow, and immaculately organized. Shoes lined the floor beneath the clothes rack. Willow walked deeper inside, scanning for the hiking boots Dale had mentioned.

Her gaze landed on the back corner, and she froze.

A gun was propped against the wall, its dark metal gleaming faintly.

Her heart slammed in her chest as fear gripped her. She couldn't be near a gun.

The thought of breaking the law, of losing everything and returning to prison, made her stomach churn. Her breath came in shallow gasps.

For ten seconds, she couldn't move. Then she turned and fled, forgetting the boots entirely.

CHAPTER TWENTY-SEVEN

FEAR'S EDGE

"**A**RE YOU OKAY?" DALE asked when he saw her running toward the trailer.

She had to look like a crazy person. Her heart pounded, and her hands trembled uncontrollably.

"There's a big gun in my grandmother's closet," she said frantically. "It can't be in the house." She tried to catch her breath. "I can't go back to prison. Please take it out of there, and you can have it."

"Whoa," he said gently, his face showing concern. "I forgot to tell you about the shotgun. That one is mine. I have Joan's inside the trailer."

He placed his hand on her shoulder.

"I was a deputy, remember?" He didn't wait for her to answer. "You can't live out here without protection. There are rattlesnakes and mountain lions. Max and Daisy are snake-trained, and we don't see many rattlers, but they're here. I find mountain lion tracks all the time. This is your property, all eighty acres of it. No one will report you, and the deputies never come out this far unless they're called and even then, it's hit and miss if they'll show."

Her pulse still raced, her mind flashing to nights locked in a cell, the constant presence of fear and control. The idea of that gun, its potential to send her back to hell, paralyzed her. She barely understood what Dale said because she could only focus on the gun.

"Hey," he said when she didn't reply. "It's okay. I understand how you feel, and it's the reason I exchanged the shotguns. Mine is registered under my name. Ballistics tests will come back to my gun. If you ever need to shoot it, it will be for a good reason. I'll take full responsibility, and I'll clear out the guns before a deputy arrives."

"Guns?" she asked as her mind slowly escaped panic mode.

"I put one of my handguns in the cellar, which I'll show you today. There's also one in a cabinet inside."

"I don't want them," Willow said stubbornly and took a step away from him.

"Okay, I get that." He looked contrite. "Think about it during our hike. If you still feel the same, I'll remove them after we return."

She exhaled shakily, her mind easing out of its spiraling fear. The idea of returning to prison still terrified her. She would rather die. A bit of what Dale said started to sink in.

"Okay," she said reluctantly.

"Do you need me to find the boots?"

She was acting like an idiot, and he was so calm.

"No, I'll grab them as long as they're not near the shotgun."

"They shouldn't be."

She walked back inside, ignored the shotgun, and found the boots. She had only the socks she'd worn the day before and put them back on. She'd gone outside in her rubber prison shower shoes, and she wanted to throw them away.

The boots fit after she tightened the laces a bit.

Max and Daisy were excited when she came outside again. Maybe they were before, but she was in such a panic she hadn't noticed.

"They know it's time for their hike," he said and whistled at the two dogs.

They turned, looked at him, then took off toward the ridge about thirty yards from the back of the house.

"If we don't follow, they'll find trouble."

The ridge actually dropped into a steep decline. A large valley rested below. It was where her grandmother wanted to plant wildflowers.

"Watch where you're going," Dale warned. "It's easy to twist an ankle. That's not a problem with the two of us, but you'll be hiking here alone before you know it. Joan checked the property lines about once a month. You don't want squatters. The dogs will be waiting in the wash, so we can go slow and steady. They like to run in the sand."

"Got it," she replied and watched her feet more closely as she walked.

"Hold up," Dale called out a minute later.

She stopped and turned in his direction. He was on one knee, looking at something on the ground.

He held up a hand so she didn't move closer.

"This is the same track I found before. I don't like that someone came up this ridge so close to the house."

"Can I see the print?" Willow asked, her curiosity overtaking her nerves.

"Circle around behind me."

She did as instructed and walked around until she peered over his shoulder.

"Look at the tread," he said, pointing at the print. "This is mine. This print is bigger than mine and much larger than yours. The cattle guys in this area wear cowboy boots. The heel makes their tread distinctive. What we're looking at is most likely athletic shoes. They're well-worn. See here, where a toe sticks out." He glanced around again, his gaze intense. "Stay behind me, and let's see how far we can track it."

The silence stretched as she followed him. Her stomach knotted. Was someone out here watching?

"Well, damn," he said about halfway to the wash. "He's good, and I'm not a professional tracker. The prints disappear here."

Dalc seemed concerned, but for her, it was fascinating to watch him work. There was something reassuring about his measured way of studying the ground, like he knew how to handle whatever might come.

He turned and looked at her.

"Be sure to take Max with you if you walk the roads or hike out here. People come up and down the wash. They sometimes get lost, but the best way to get shot is to walk up behind someone's home. The people out here don't take kindly to strangers. If you accidentally find yourself on someone's property, tell them you're Joan's granddaughter, you're lost, and you're staying at her place. Most will help you if you have a right to be here."

The dogs came running, panting and excited. Max sniffed the ground where the last track was found and then ran back toward the wash with Daisy following.

"Is he tracking the smell?" Willow asked.

Dale smiled and shook his head.

"He's never been trained, and neither has Daisy. I've seen them chasing rabbits, and while they're attacking a shrub, the rabbit hightails it in the other direction. They don't figure it out most of the time and destroy the bush before they give up. Right now, they're impatient for us to join them."

They made it to the wash. Willow bent down and picked up a handful of sand with a questioning look.

"Millions of years ago," Dale said, "this wasn't land at all. You'll find seashells and sometimes shell fossils buried in the rocks. Joan collected them along with various stones and petrified wood. We have jasper, quartz, and a bunch of others. Joan has a few books on them. The area out the back door holds an assortment of what she found. She also searched the anthills for anthill garnets. She showed me a few of them. Small but pretty. They're most likely in the house somewhere."

Willow turned the sand over in her hand. The idea that something so small and overlooked could hold such beauty stirred something in her.

"About the shotgun," Dale said. "I know it worries you, but you need something in the house. I'll need to hitch up today and go back to my property."

"Do you have a lot of work to do there?"

"Goodness, no. It's a barren piece of land that fit my budget. Not a lot I can do with it. I thought I would eventually build a house, but I'm getting old and don't mind the trailer."

"Move here permanently," Willow said, trying to keep fear out of her voice. She didn't like showing she was afraid of anything.

He looked at her and smiled.

"You're young. Eventually, you'll meet some people in town and make friends. You don't need an old man like me hanging around."

"I'll pay you," she said desperately.

"None of that. What's really bothering you?" he asked gently.

Her gaze roamed the area.

"It's too big and wide open," she said when she met his eyes again. Dammit, she just needed to admit it. "I've never been alone, and I've never made friends. You can live here forever, and I won't get tired of you being here. I'll even keep the shotgun in the closet."

He looked at her for a long time, and she thought he would refuse.

"I reckon I can stay. It's possible Daisy would go into a deep state of depression without Max, so I'll do it for her."

"The same would happen to Max," she said in relief. "We don't want that."

Dale stayed, and Willow's new life began.

Chapter Twenty-Eight

Photographic Memories

WILLOW TOOK TIME TO go through her grandmother's closet. It was harder than she thought. In a box marked, Willow, she found a handwritten note from her grandmother.

Dearest Willow, your mother never told me where she lived, and the post marks came from different states, so I figured she moved around. I have treasured each image of you, and some day, I hope you find it in your heart to forgive your mother. I've kept her letters for you to read and you will notice them time warn. I reread them at least once a year. Love, your grandmother who loves you more than life.

Willow wiped away her tears and searched the box. Most photos were Willow, baby through toddler years, and then more sporadic from once a year to one every two years, up until Willow turned twelve and they stopped. Willow didn't want to remember the years from twelve to fifteen, so it was oddly comforting that there were none. She had never seen the photos. After going through the pictures, she stored them on a high shelf, so they were out of sight. One day, when she was stronger, she would read the letters.

The underground shelter was next on her list. She loved the ingenious swing-away door that covered the storage below. There were additional supplies such as canned food, and five-gallon drums of water. The handgun Dale warned her about was attached to the side wall with tools and several knives. The blades were the defensive kind and something she couldn't afford to be caught with. She found a sheath for the smaller of the three, and decided she would wear it on the property. It worked better for her than carrying a gun.

Next came Lucy. Her grandmother had named the truck after the *I Love Lucy* show. She decided to take her out the first time without Dale, determined to do something by herself. Unfortunately, the clutch was beyond her. Dale smiled when she told him, stopped what he was doing, and showed her what was up. Lucy huffed and puffed for her inadequate driver, stalling repeatedly, and causing tears to fill Willow's eyes at her inability.

Dale couldn't keep a smile off his face. "There are a handful of farm kids that can drive a stick," he told her. It takes finesse and power because she's old and they didn't make it easy back then. Keep trying and eventually you'll find the balance. If it were easy, they'd call it knowing, and not learning." He walked off whistling.

It took three days before she could get Lucy out of the barn. Willow didn't stop there and drove her to the dirt road north of the property. After only one stall, Willow felt she'd conquered the beast. Dale took her out weekly and gave her instructions on the rules of the road.

Three months flew by.

Have you considered getting a name change," Dale asked, over dinner one night.

"Change my name?" she questioned.

"I'm talking about your last name. Willow kind of works for you, but I thought it might be nice for you to have a new beginning. You can change both if you like or keep what you have."

"I didn't know it was possible," she said, while thinking about the idea.

"It takes a superior court judge," he stopped because he had to have seen the look on her face. "I would be with you every step of the way if you decide to do it."

"I'll think about it," she said.

That was one of the nicest things about Dale. He gave her room to make mistakes and didn't pry too deeply.

Within twenty-four hours she knew she wanted to change her name. Dale looked into exactly what needed doing to make it happen. The first being a valid ID. Willow took the driver's tests and passed though she was more nervous than she expected. Dale printed the paperwork she needed from an online site and helped her fill it out for her new name.

"What did you decide to call yourself?" he asked.

The smile she gave him was maybe the happiest she had shown. "Willow Joan Morgan," she said.

"Perfect."

Neither said anything about the tears that welled in his eyes.

On her assigned court date, she went before the superior judge, Dale at her side, and the request was granted. He also agreed to seal the name change record.

"Good luck, Ms. Morgan," the judge told her with genuine warmth, and she went from

Willow Gail Humphrey to Willow Joan Morgan. She took the paperwork to MVD, and they told her it could take up to two weeks before her new license arrived.

Dale brought the mail from town, with her license in it.

"This calls for a celebration, Ms. Morgan. I say we pop another bottle of wine open, and I'll make a special dinner."

"Only if I have salad duty," she said with a laugh and smile that wouldn't leave her face.

For the first time, she drank three glasses of wine over dinner, and stumbled into bed tipsy after Dale went to his trailer. It had been a great day.

Max's low growl woke her. His large snout pointed toward the window beside her bed.

A strange face peered inside.

Chapter Twenty-Nine

Bearded Mush Face

HIS FACE WAS MASHED against the screen, a beard covering the lower half. Willow had just begun turning the lights off at night because they attracted too many small, flying critters through the screen, or he would have been able to see her clearly without needing to be so close.

Fear gripped her at the same time Max jumped on the bed and gave a deep throaty bark. The man disappeared. Her hand went out, reaching for the cell phone, and shakily, she called Dale's number.

He answered on the first ring.

"There's a man outside. He was looking in my bedroom window." Max continued to growl in the background

"Daisy started up about thirty seconds ago. I'm coming over. Open the door when I knock but keep Max inside with you. Daisy will stay inside with you too."

Dale knocked two minutes later. Willow unlocked the screen. He held a large flashlight and shined it around the property half looking at her and half keeping an eye out behind him. His gray hair stood up on one side and lay flat on the other. He wore his wrinkled shirt from the day before, and a gun holstered on his hip held up by belted blue jeans. It was three in the morning, and he looked tired.

"I'm going to scout around the house and barn," he said. "Keep the dogs inside with you."

"What about calling the sheriff?" she asked, fear rising in her voice.

He turned and looked at her. "I'm retired, but this was my area, and I rarely had backup. Tonight, I have you and two large dogs. Make some coffee, and if I'm not back in ten minutes, call 911. Now lock the doors behind me."

He didn't give her time to argue. Willow started coffee, her hands shaking so hard, she worried she would break the glass carafe. This was worse than prison when guards would stare at her and creep her out. She had just begun to feel safe in her grandmother's house. Her hands continued to tremble as she grabbed two mugs and kept an eye on the clock. Dale knocked on the door six minutes after he left.

"Let me in?" he said, and she quickly unlocked both doors. Dale's light continued to shine into the night.

"What is it?" she asked when she saw his expression.

"The footprints outside your window match the ones we've seen around the property. It's got to be one of the locals which I don't like at all. There's enough crazy out here to fill a bar on free whiskey night. Whoever he is, he's turning into a problem. How clearly could you see him?"

"Not well. He had a bushy beard along with a mushed nose and lips."

"Mushed nose and lips?" he questioned, a slight grin appearing at the corners of his mouth.

She simply nodded.

"Seeing a beard means you've eliminated the women, but included every man who lives out here accept me." Dale shaved each morning, and she rarely saw a sign of facial hair.

"Are you calling the sheriff now?" she asked.

"Let's have coffee and talk about that. There are some things you need to know, and I've been waiting for the right time to explain," he said, grim-faced.

With coffee in hand, Dale settled on the reclining chair, and Willow took the couch. Max and Daisy lay down and didn't seem concerned about anyone outside. It allowed Willow to relax.

Dale cleared his throat, looked away from her, and began talking. "Joan was considered a thorn in the sheriff department's side. I ran a bit of interference and handled just about all her complaints. She was a smart woman, and I, as a deputy, irritated the crap out of her." He still didn't meet Willow's eyes. "You said she told you about the court hearing with the puppy mill and how Jeb Hogg got away without charges?"

Willow nodded, but he still wasn't looking at her, so she said, "Yes."

"A few months before all hell broke loose at the Hogg homestead, one of the investigators from the county drug task force approached me. They're a ragtag team from every department in the county. Each department loans an officer for a three-year stint. It's usually someone they want out of their hair. The investigator explained that the Hoggs were under investigation as a major methamphetamine distributor and most likely cooking it on the property." Dale stopped for a moment, and Willow saw the sadness he tried to hide. It was in his voice too. He took a sip of coffee and continued. "Joan was making a fuss about the dog fighting again. She'd stopped trusting me to do anything, so she took her complaints straight to the front office and filed in writing." Dale pulled a silver flask from his pocket and poured some into his mug. "Liquid courage," he said and finally looked at her. "Would you like some?"

Willow shook her head.

"Joan's complaints were valid, but there are only two deputies handling over five hundred square miles. I checked on her because I live out here. If I had lived in town, I wouldn't have, and that shames me." He took a longer pull from the mug. "The people here on the ranch keep to themselves. Some are like me and were short on money needing a cheap place to live, or like Joan, wanting to escape something personal. Others have more nefarious reasons. They're running from child support or much worse. We have Sovereign Citizens. They're a crazy group that believe the sheriff is the highest legitimate law enforcement because sheriffs are elected by the people at the will of the people. They don't feel that way about local police and consider them an extension of an illegitimate government." He shrugged. "Local police are trained to call for deputy backup if they run into them. SCs won't acquire ID, and don't register or insure their vehicles. For the most part, they're left alone, and that's why they stay."

He took another long drink and stood to refill his mug. "Do you need a warmup?" he asked.

Again, Willow shook her head.

He refilled his mug, added more liquor, and sat back in the chair. "Long story short, the people here leave you alone if you leave them alone. Joan didn't follow the rules when it came to the Hoggs. The last time she complained to me, there was nothing I could do because of the meth investigation. I tried to pacify her, and that just made her angrier. I couldn't tell her what was going on without risking my job, so I stayed quiet." He took another drink.

"About ten years ago," he continued, "Someone found a body in an old trailer here on the ranch. The man had been dead for two to three years and his body was mummified. There was little investigation. I decided to look into it myself and questioned the people in the area. That didn't go well, because like I said, the people out here mind their own business. Someone made a complaint, and I was called into my commander's office. Very explicitly, I was told to do as much work as possible off the ranch and to leave the dead body investigation alone."

Willow could tell this angered him.

"After what happened the night Joan died, they found evidence of a major meth lab in the Hoggs' barn." He paused for a moment, his face remaining grim. "I have no idea how long the drug investigation had been going on, and it could have been years. The narc investigators don't trust others, and personally, I didn't trust them. Too many opportunities to hide large amounts of cash, and let corruption lead them down a hellhole. If I had disregarded what they told me, and said something to Joan, she would be alive today."

Dale leaned forward and looked Willow straight in the eyes. "I'm the reason your grandmother died."

Bottom of Form

CHAPTER THIRTY

SOUR TRUTH

WILLOW TRIED TO ABSORB what Dale told her. She'd listened to her grandmother gripe about the Hoggs, Dale, and other law enforcement. Willow hated to admit it, but she enjoyed the stories. They were life on the outside, and she replayed them in her head each night when she couldn't sleep, which was often.

She didn't feel Dale was responsible for her grandmother's death. Though what he'd told her explained a lot. He was so good to her, and she'd known it had to be more than loving her grandmother. It was his guilt, and she wasn't sure how she felt about it. Instead of tackling the issues that would make him feel better right now, she decided to open up to him. He deserved the truth too.

"I killed my father," she said.

He nodded. "I know that."

"He abused my mother physically. He did more than that to me." She looked down. "My mother found out and she snapped. She went after him with a bat. He beat her to death with his bare hands. I hated him. I told my lawyer what really happened that night. He said I needed to keep it to myself. My grandmother never knew the truth." She looked into her cup, then back at Dale. "I think I'll try some of your nerve-calming juice," she said.

Dale handed the flask over, and she poured in about half of what he'd put in his mug. She handed the silver container back and took a sip. She choked. A small grin appeared on Dale's lips, which made it worth it.

When she had her breathing under control, she continued. "My lawyer claimed self-defense, but the jury didn't buy it because they were right. My dad killed my mom, but afterward, he curled up on the floor and cried. He even told me to call the police. Instead, I took a baseball bat and beat him to death. I got the sentence I deserved. I just never wanted to disappoint my grandmother because she had her own guilt. She didn't even know my dad had moved us back to Arizona. I was the only person she had, and she was the same for me. I never planned to tell her."

"Your dad got exactly what he deserved. I would do it for you if we could go back. Why are you telling me?" he asked gently.

"We can't go back. Maybe my grandmother would be alive, and maybe she wouldn't. If what happened with my dad happened again, I would kill him, even knowing my fate."

It took Dale a moment, and then he smiled. "We're quite the pair, aren't we?"

"I thought you would look at me like a murderer," she said, refusing to let tears form in her eyes.

He stood and sat beside her on the couch. "I never had a daughter. You're too young for that, but I do think of you as my granddaughter. I definitely love you like one."

In Willow's entire life, only her grandmother had told her she was loved. There was no stopping the tears now. Dale wrapped his arms around her and let her cry. When she gained control, he pulled away and looked at her.

"Can you forgive me for not being there for Joan?" he asked.

"There's nothing to forgive. Is this why you retired?"

"There were lots of reasons, but what happened with Joan was very high on the list." He paused for a moment. "After this incident with the peeping Tom, you need to learn to shoot. We're going to the range tomorrow. As your grandfather, I have the right to make demands occasionally, and you have the right to tell me to jump in a creek. I won't be around forever, and you need to know how to defend yourself with more than a baseball bat."

Dale didn't hate her. He didn't look at her like a monster. He even teased her about using a baseball bat, which she never thought she would smile at. But she did and nodded. "Okay, but I'm not happy about learning to shoot, and I'll probably be horrible at it. I don't want to accidentally kill you or one of the dogs."

"Women are naturally more gifted at shooting than men. You'll do fine."

"What are you going to do about the man at the window?"

"You and I are going to track him if you're willing. We're not professionals, but we'll find him."

"You sure you don't want to call the sheriff's department?" She asked carefully.

"They won't do anything." Steel shone in his eyes.

"I'll learn to shoot, and help you follow his tracks. I want to feel safe and right now, I don't."

"We'll change that," Dale said.

As soon as the sun came up, they locked the dogs inside the house, and Dale drove her to the range.

"The berm is used by the locals. It's not an actual shooting range, but safety applies with all guns no matter where you are."

He went through his safety rules as he drove. Everything he said seemed logical. A gun was always loaded, even if you just removed the bullets. Never point a gun unless you plan to shoot it. His last bit of advice made her smile.

"If you do need to shoot a human being, make sure there's only one person alive to give their side of the story." He held up his hand. "I know that didn't work for you at fifteen, but you have good instincts, and I have no problem that you killed a man who deserved it. We're not the judge and jury, but sometimes you need to take a stand. I'm proud of you for taking yours."

He unloaded the equipment and guns after they arrived at the berm.

"I'll show you how to clean them when we get home. Let's see what you've got."

He set up a few metal targets. He stapled a paper one between two wooden props covered in cardboard. After securing eye and ear protection that made her feel silly, he walked her through firing, ejecting the magazine, and inserting a new one. When it was time to aim, she had more confidence than she thought she'd have.

It took a few adjustments before she hit the target, and that was outside the outer circle. Within ten minutes, she was hitting the target each time. Dale moved her farther back, and they started again. Her confidence grew with each round.

"They make small pea-shooter .22s that can be carried in a pocket," Dale said. "I don't recommend them, but if you're uncomfortable having something showing on your hip or carrying the shotgun, we can compromise. They would most likely hurt a rattler. The noise might even scare off a mountain lion."

She couldn't keep the smile off her face when it came time to learn about the shotgun. Dale had been right. Learning to shoot made her feel calmer about guns. Not safer, but more aware. She would keep the shotgun in her grandmother's closet. With a little prodding, she might wear a handgun on her hip, but that was for another day.

It took an hour to clean everything, including the magazines, once they were home. She almost forgot about the man at the window.

Almost.

Chapter Thirty-One

Fear the Bitch

TWO MONTHS WENT BY with no sign of the peeping Tom, as Dale now called him. Willow began to feel safe again. She hiked the property with the dogs and the shotgun when Dale was too busy to come with her. She still felt uncomfortable about the shotgun being a felony for her to carry, but safety over road her fear. She watched for tracks and occasionally found some cowboy boot prints. They didn't bother her, and none of those prints came close to the house. She ran into cows from time to time and saw a golden eagle, which made her long for a camera. The shot she took with her phone wasn't as good as her grandmother's photography.

She learned small lessons by making mistakes. If the front door was left open, mice made their home inside. She hated the idea of killing them, but Dale told her that hantavirus was a big deal in the high desert and once they came into the house, they had to be eliminated. He ordered zap traps after telling her the glue ones were inhumane. They couldn't use poison because of the dogs. After killing the first one, she learned to keep the door shut.

Louisa and Roger, the couple with the horses, rode over one day to introduce themselves. They were in their sixties. Louisa had dark skin, brown hair, some of the whitest teeth Willow had ever seen, and a smile that never stopped. Roger, more serious, had short gray hair and a large belly, which Louisa said came from her cooking. Louisa invited Willow to come have coffee and see their hay bale home when she had extra time.

Willow was nervous meeting them at first, but her anxiety melted away quickly. Dale called them good people, and with everything he'd said about others on the ranch, Louisa and Roger were the best neighbors to have.

They'd ridden the horses and introduced them to Willow. She fell in love. She had no plans to buy one, but Louisa said she should help Dale care for them when they were out of town. He'd offered when Louisa and Roger first arrived, and she called him her godsend.

Willow planned to visit them after harvest season. Gardening had become her favorite pastime. Her grandmother had logged everything, which made understanding soil, humidity, and composting easier. She had also stored seed packets with instructions. Eating what she grew was a huge reward for Willow.

She was also learning to cook. Dale told her everything was delicious, but she learned to recognize when he was being kind. They laughed about it, and she went back to the drawing board to try again.

He left early one morning to drive to the city for supplies. It was the first time Willow was alone at the house. She decided to take Max and Daisy for a hike. She walked through the wash to the other side and headed in a direction she took on a regular basis. The dogs ran ahead, weaving in and out of the undergrowth while playing.

Willow decided to take a break on a large boulder and had just sat down for water when she heard a clang and a sharp cry from Daisy. They were about twenty yards away, though she couldn't see them until she was closer.

A metal-jawed trap held Daisy's paw. Max paced around her, stopped, sniffed his friend's foot, and growled. Willow panicked. She had no idea what to do. She tried her cell phone, but there was no signal. Her heart pounded and her vision narrowed until black edges crept in. Max's sudden bark snapped her out of it. He stood facing her, as if he knew she needed help. After several slow, even breaths the world came back into focus. She had to save Daisy.

Whoever did this, staked the trap into the ground. She had no idea what they used to hold it in place, but it wouldn't budge. Daisy whined pathetically and Willow wanted to cry at her inability to help. She thought of her grandmother's capacity to adapt. A steady calm came over her. She was Joan's granddaughter. Giving up was not an option and allowing Daisy to suffer wasn't either.

Daisy's large eyes looked into hers with trust and absolute knowledge that Willow would help.

"I'll get you out, my beautiful girl," she promised.

She examined the trap, while Daisy and Max waited calmly. There were levers on the sides, and if she were understanding how it worked, she needed to push down on both levers. She pressed one, but like the anchor, it didn't budge. Looking around, she saw a rock and grabbed it. Using her boot on one lever and the rock on the other, she tried again. They gave a little. With a burst of adrenaline, she put as much force as she could into it. The jaws opened, and Daisy pulled free.

Blood covered Willow's hands, and for a moment, she had a flashback to killing her father. Max licked her face, and once more, she was able to snap out of it.

"Can you walk, girl?" Willow asked softly as she rubbed her head.

Daisy let out a pathetic whine and licked her hand, taking some of the blood with it. Willow gave her a few minutes and used the time to look around. Her heart nearly stopped when she noticed a print in the dirt. It was the peeping Tom.

"Don't panic," she said aloud. "You have the shotgun, and Max has four good legs." She searched the area and didn't find another trap or more prints.

When she felt Daisy was ready, she walked ahead to see if she would follow. Limping and mostly using three legs, Daisy managed the hike back to the house with help from Willow on the steeper inclines.

When they came over the last ridge, Willow saw the barn.

BITCH was painted in large red letters, covering one entire side.

She quickly got the dogs inside the house, locked the security screens, and bolted the heavy wooden doors in front and back. Her hands shook as she called Dale.

"Hey, what's up?" he asked. "You miss this old man already?"

The words spilled out, and she wasn't even sure if she was coherent.

"Stay put," he said. "Call Louisa and Roger. Don't open the door until you hear their voices. I'm turning around, but it will be at least an hour before I get back. If that asshole puts his face to a window, shoot him. We'll deal with the consequences later. Do you understand?" he demanded.

She'd never heard him this angry.

"I will, I promise."

"Drink some water and give some to the dogs. Use the first aid kit Joan put together and do the best you can. The fact Daisy walked out is a good sign. The traps aren't meant to snap legs, but sometimes they do. Most of all, stay safe. Call Louisa and Roger right now."

"I will. Don't kill yourself getting here."

"I won't, but don't hold me to not killing that son of a bitch when I find him."

Louisa didn't answer when Willow called, so she left a message, trying to sound calmer than she felt. Daisy allowed her to clean the wounds and wrap her leg. Afterward, she lay quietly, her pathetic eyes following Willow. Her sadness broke Willow's heart. Dale had told her about the abuse Daisy suffered at the hands of the Hoggs. She had the scars that proved it, and she also shied if you moved too quickly around her.

For the first time since she'd killed her father, Willow wanted to hurt someone.

Chapter Thirty-Two

Reality Sucks

Ten minutes after Willow left a message for Louisa, she called. "We're in the valley for a doctor's appointment," Louisa said. "Is Daisy okay?"

Willow hadn't told her about the writing on the barn. "She's doing better," Willow answered honestly. "Dale is on his way back, and we'll be okay until he returns."

"Is the leg broken?"

Dale had told Willow that Louisa was a rancher's wife, and there were no tougher women born on this earth.

"I don't think so, just deep cuts, but in one, I can see bone. Dale will know more about it than me. Daisy seems comfortable for now."

"Give her two aspirin if it's not bleeding heavily."

"I wrapped it, but no blood is showing on the outside. I'll give her the aspirin."

"Okay. Call if you have questions and send a text when Dale gets there."

"I will, promise. And thank you for calling me back."

"We gotta stick together. I'll let the ranch board know that someone put out a leghold trap. They're illegal, and we'll find who did this. They better hope it's not me who comes across them first. He won't have a strip of skin left on his backside."

That made Willow smile.

"They're calling Roger to the back, so I gotta go."

"I'll text as soon as Dale is here," Willow said.

After disconnecting, she walked to the bedroom window that looked out at the barn. Who would do this? Her father had no family, or at least none who claimed him. Willow didn't know anyone around but Dale, Louisa, and Roger. She'd said hello to a few people in town but hadn't made conversation.

She thought about prison. Because she kept to herself, she was considered conceited. A few of the older inmates stuck up for her because they knew she'd been inside since she was fifteen. Willow couldn't imagine one of the idiots who tried to provoke her coming up here to terrorize her. They were women, and the print was larger than Dale's shoes. It made no sense. She didn't understand how she could have made an enemy.

An hour later, Dale's truck rolled up. She sent a quick text to Louisa, unlocked the door, and ran outside. Dale pulled her into his arms, but she'd seen the look on his face when his eyes caught the painting on the barn.

"You're okay," he murmured against her hair. "I promise that son of a bitch won't be." His hold cut her panic in half.

Daisy limped outside and slowly made her way to Dale. He leaned over and picked her up, carrying her back inside the house. His angry expression didn't change.

He called the sheriff's department. Three hours later, a deputy arrived to take a report. He was young, maybe Willow's age, and he showed no compassion for Daisy's run-in with the trap. He also didn't want Max anywhere near him, so Willow had to take the dog inside.

The deputy didn't stay long.

"That moron was a wet-behind-the-ears rookie when I left. Now he's an arrogant prick." Dale's face reddened. "Pardon my choice of words," he said.

Willow smiled more to relieve Dale's worry than for herself.

"The deputy barely paid attention when I told him about the shoeprint and peeping Tom," he continued. "The entire department is worthless."

Louisa and Roger showed up soon after the deputy left. Louisa examined Daisy.

"She's lucky," Louisa assured them. "Those traps can really injure an animal. I hunt, but I'd never use one of those things, they're evil."

Dale slept in the house that night. He used the pullout couch, which had to be uncomfortable, though he didn't complain.

"We need to order a bed," she told him the next morning while they drank coffee. "We can put it in the office so you have privacy. I'll move some clothes and boxes out of the closet and store them in the barn loft so you can have space for your personal things."

He gave her a long, assessing look. "You'll get tired of me before you know it."

Willow walked over, sat beside him, and rested her head on his shoulder. "You're my grandpa. I'll never get tired of you."

"Don't make an old goat cry," he muttered, placing his arm around her and squeezing. They sat like that for several moments.

"We need to talk," he said. "I may know who this is."

Willow pulled away and stared at him.

"One of the Hogg sons was never found," he began. "There's no one else it could be. You practically never leave here, and when you do, I'm with you. You get stares from some of the men in town—"

Willow shook her head.

"Don't give me that. It's normal for a pretty girl to get looks. When the man's too old, I give him a look of my own. But anyway, the Hogg kid is the culprit. I was a deputy, and I'm sorry it took me this long to figure it out. I bet he's staying in one of the deserted homesteads. He's probably not far from here. I'll head out tonight and scout around."

Willow panicked. "You can't leave me here alone at night. We need to call the deputy back. It's their job. They can look for him."

"I wish it was that simple. They don't care about the people out here and call us cedar rats. I've always hated that name. Sure, we have our share of weirdos, but we also have people like Roger, Louisa, and you. The name cedar rats is derogatory on purpose, but that's the local cops for you. The force leaches humanity out of the best of us."

He stopped for a moment, and she could tell he was thinking about a bad memory.

"Two years before I retired, a man beat up his wife. It was one of the few times I was with another deputy. It quickly became apparent, when interviewing the three women in the home, that something was off. The deputy with me asked belligerently, 'Is this one of those plural wife situations?' The three women froze and clammed up, refusing to say another word. If I hadn't been there, the man wouldn't have been arrested. Other deputies gave me flack for getting involved in their marital situation.

"I could care less that a man lived with three women, if he treated them well. Basically, none of my business. The consensus at the department was the women chose him and could live with their choice."

He paused in his rant, sadness taking over his expression. "I allowed so many things to slide when I shouldn't have. My maker will judge me accordingly."

Dale had never even mentioned a belief in God, and it shook Willow for a moment. She leaned back into him, placing her arms around his shoulders, breathing in the scent of the aftershave he always wore.

"Your maker will see everything you've done for me. We have time to make up for our wrongs. If you move in here, we can watch over each other. I don't know what I would have done after my grandmother died if it weren't for you. Each day, I feel luckier than the day before."

Willow took a long breath, her decision made. "If you go out tonight, I go with you." Her voice held the same stubbornness as Joan's.

Dale gave a huge, overly dramatic sigh. "Just like your grandmother. The apple don't fall far from the tree."

She didn't know exactly what that meant, but she got the drift.

They ate breakfast, and when they finished, Dale went to the barn to tackle the graffiti. Willow cleaned the dishes, then straightened the small office so a bed would fit. She would need Dale's help to move the desk out. It wasn't exactly heavy, but it was bulky. Things would be safer once he moved inside the house. He was thinking short term, while Willow was determined he would live out his life with her.

She'd never had a true friend or a grandfather. Her dad's parents disowned him after he attacked his father and put him in the hospital. Willow's attorney contacted them before the trial. They never replied. Her grandmother was the only one who cared, and now there was Dale.

By the time she went outside, Dale had the first coat of paint covering the hate.

"After another coat, you won't see it at all," he told her.

"How is Daisy doing?" she asked.

"She's limping, but the wound looks good. She may be milking it."

Willow laughed. "I don't blame her. The trap scared me half to death."

He came off the ladder. "We're going to find this guy and stop him. Louisa and Roger have watched the dogs before, and they won't mind doing it again. I don't want Max or Daisy running into another trap."

"I'm ready whenever you are," she said. "Are we scouting tonight?"

"No, tomorrow morning when the sun comes up is soon enough. I'll call Roger and tell him we'll put the dogs in his barn, so we don't wake them."

"I cleared out some things from the office. Can you help me move the desk?"

"You're sure about this?" Dale looked skeptical.

"I'm sure. I'd like it to be a permanent arrangement. My cooking is better, and I can take over the meals."

"If we do this, we'll share meals and cleanup. You have a lot to learn about taking care of the property."

"I doubt I'll ever know as much as you."

Dale laughed. "Joan beat us both. There was nothing that darned woman couldn't learn. I complained about a problem with my well pump once, and she told me exactly what the problem was without looking at it. I have a feeling you'll surpass her."

"I doubt it," Willow muttered, which only made Dale's smile widen.

Dale insisted on paying for his new bed but told Willow to order it. He handed over his bank card.

"What's your spending limit?" she asked him.

He actually blushed, then shuffled his feet for about ten seconds. "I'm getting up there, and it would be nice to have one of those fancy beds that I could read in while sitting upright. If you call it a medical bed, I'll move back into the trailer."

She shook her head at how ridiculous he was and purposely hid her smile. "I'll order a medical bed."

Dale cussed a few times. She heard him mutter, "Dang blasted woman is Joan incarnate," as he walked out the door. Willow went to the computer and started searching.

Chapter Thirty-Three

Vengeance of the Hogg

LANCE WAITED WEEKS FOR the bitch to be alone. She looked like her grandmother, and he owed her for everything the old woman had done to his family. He thought of her as the bitch because she looked too big for her britches, and she had everything he wanted.

After his father went crazy and shot his mother and brothers, Lance ran into the desert to escape. Before he left, he'd carried his mom to her bed. He'd mostly felt sorry for her because she was about as worthless as they came. He'd liked Carrie, though, and was pissed at his da for killing her.

He hadn't understood the insanity of that night until he'd had a chance to think about it. Rabies was the obvious culprit, and his mind came up with the excuse that it was the old woman's fault. She'd caused trouble since they moved in. He wished he could have killed her himself.

He'd watched from a high ridge, far enough away but close enough to see when the police arrived. He'd seen the barn explode, which really pissed him off. They had another large meth order to fulfill and had already been paid. The money burned up in the house. Their buyer would kill him, so he decided to lay low.

It wasn't easy. He'd lost weight, been eaten by mosquitoes, and his only water supply came from the water mill the cows used. He had cuts and scrapes covering him, along with constant head and body aches. Two teeth had fallen out, and another was loose. His goal was to kill the old man, who had been a cop, and take over the property. His da's place was destroyed, and there was nothing left for him.

He'd decided to rattle them first. It was most likely stupid, but he couldn't help it. He didn't have a gun, though he'd managed to steal a good-sized hunting knife. His da had always called him worthless, but who was worthless now? He'd been the only one left standing.

As part of his plan to terrorize, he'd stolen paint from a storage shed a few miles away. He stayed in a deserted homestead that had been abandoned years before. It was little more than a shack and didn't have much inside, but it did have the metal traps, which enabled him to catch rabbits. He'd stolen blankets from another place and got lucky one night when he found a Dutch oven at a homestead a mile away. The only person out here who called the cops had been the old lady, so he felt relatively safe that he wouldn't be caught stealing what he needed.

Each month, when he couldn't stand his smell any longer, he'd sneak over to the water mill at night and bathe. At first, he liked being on his own. The cold had gotten bad, and he almost froze to death several times. He wanted to kill the cop, just so he could use his place to get warm. He worried about his cop friends though. He got sick several times and that most likely started because he lit wood fires inside the shack with little ventilation. He'd survived two winters and now all he could think of was the bitch and what he would do to her.

She would change everything. After he beat her up some, she would do what he said. The old man would die, but he would keep the bitch alive until she no longer pleased him.

That could take a while because he was horny just thinking about her. Sometimes his thoughts didn't make sense, but he'd been that way his whole life. His da said he was the dumbest of the bunch.

He put his hand between his legs and made himself feel better.

The bitch would be doing it soon.

CHAPTER THIRTY-FOUR

CROSSING THE LINE

WILLOW COULDN'T HELP BUT dwell on the ramifications of going after Lance Hogg. She'd never regretted killing her father. She was twenty-five now. Could she kill a stranger? She didn't think so. It wasn't just the threat of prison; it was who she had become. Killing was wrong. As Dale said, she was not the judge and jury.

Dale started coffee at four in the morning. She heard him moving around the kitchen and went out to speak with him about the thoughts that had kept her up all night. He listened to everything she said.

"Just because I hung up my badge doesn't mean I plan to break the law," he told her. A small quirk formed on his lips. "There are very few lines I'll cross so don't blame me for the guns that go against the law for you. In a few years, you'll be able to apply to get your rights back. No person in their right mind would think twice about you having protection out here," he continued. "Lance Hogg has an active warrant. I want him to pay for his crimes legally. The meth lab will likely get him ten years. The jaw trap and even the painting on the barn are minor offenses and will get him a slap on the wrist. I'm going after him because the sheriff's department won't. My plan is to deliver him very much alive. If he has a bruise or two, I won't have any idea how it happened."

He took her hand. "I've never killed a man, though I've had to think long and hard about it. My job meant it could happen. I won't throw away the years I gave to law enforcement for prison. I will, however, protect us. You need to have your head right, or I don't want you with me. Looking for Lance Hogg is dangerous, and it's no reason to die."

Willow had killed a man, but he left that unsaid. She was okay with Dale's reasoning, and she had no problem protecting him. She needed to feel safe. As long as Lance was out there, she wasn't.

"I'm going with you," she said with a cold look that told Dale she meant business.

His answering nod said he understood.

Louisa and Roger were waiting for them when they arrived, an hour before dawn.

"Do you want to take the horses?" Roger asked.

"No," Dale said. "More traps worry me, and we don't need a horse going down. Going on foot is our best bet."

Neither Louisa nor Roger asked why they weren't calling the sheriff's department. They'd had a few things stolen, and no one ever showed up to take a report. Dale figured it was the Hogg kid but kept it to himself.

"We're going to drive about five miles out and walk in from there. We have our phones if we run into trouble. We'll both be armed too."

"Should we expect you before dark?" Louisa asked.

"Yes, you should," he assured her.

Louisa gave Willow a quick hug. "Don't let this old man get you into trouble you can't handle. We'll come out if we need to."

Willow squeezed her back and followed Dale to his truck. Lucy stayed in the barn at home because she was old, and he wanted something more trustworthy.

"They're good people," Dale said as they drove away from Louisa and Roger.

Willow's nerves were on edge, and she hadn't spoken much since their conversation over coffee.

"You're sure you want to do this?" Dale asked, giving her a side-eye as he drove over the bumpy dirt road.

"You keep asking, and my answer stays the same."

"Then what's eating you?" he muttered.

She shrugged. "Some of it's anger over Daisy, mostly. I've also been thinking about my grandmother and what drove her to risk her life. She had been angry at the Hoggs for years. It was mostly because of Carrie. I sometimes thought she watched out for Carrie because she was unable to watch out for me."

"Joan let me have it more than once when it came to Carrie," Dale said. "I tried, but even when child services questioned her, she wouldn't say anything. She had a few scrapes, but those could be put down to a normal active childhood. There were no signs of obvious abuse. Like so many other children, homeschooling made it harder. If a teacher had seen her daily, it might have changed things. Joan is up there ranting at me still because I failed that little girl. I studied the evidence from the night Joan died. She was on a mission to save Carrie, and she gave her life to do it. Carrie had rabies but that's not what killed her. That little girl was beaten to death, and I should have done more." He glanced at Willow. "Your grandmother would be very proud of you."

"Thank you," Willow replied before she switched subjects. She wanted her grandmother to be proud, but praise made her uncomfortable. "What's your plan?"

"I want to set ground rules," Dale said.

"I'm all ears," she said grumpily, which made him smile.

"The guns are registered to me. I'm wearing an ankle holster for the one you're carrying. It will look like I took it as backup. If I'm down and you need to shoot, don't hesitate. I still say taking him alive is the goal, but we can't be stupid about it."

"Is that why you put rope in the backpack?"

"It's exactly why. I have handcuffs in the trailer, but that would look like we went to catch him and won't look good to a judge. We're searching for traps. That's our story, and we're sticking to it. If we find Lance and something bad happens, stay silent when the deputies ask questions. I read your court transcript. That detective hounded you for hours, and you were just a kid. You didn't say much, but there were inconsistencies in your story. Your lawyer was right to have you keep the truth to yourself. If a cop is taken into custody, they know to say nothing."

"I never cared one way or another about cops until I met you," Willow said. "Are you the only good cop left?"

He chuckled. "If I'm a good one, this world is in sad shape. Out here, far away from the city, the pay is low, and they don't have many people signing up for the job. Half of them who do don't make it through the background check required by the state. When they do pass the first part, another half fail in the academy. If I knew what I know now, I would have chosen a different career."

Willow slowly felt herself unwinding.

"You ready?" Dale asked as he slowed the truck, pulled off the road, and rolled to a stop.

"Any more words of wisdom?" she asked.

"Stay alive. He will be armed. Maybe not with a gun, but he'll have something. He's not thinking right either. Be prepared for anything."

"Yes, Grandpa," Willow said.

"Smartass," he said but she saw the pride he felt when she called him that.

Dale carried the backpack, and Willow had two water bottles in the pockets of a pair of pants she'd taken from her grandmother's closet. She'd never gotten around to buying her own things because Joan's fit, and there were enough to last her for years.

"You know where we are, don't you?" Willow asked after looking around.

"We're five miles past my place. I worked this area, remember?"

She nodded. The landscape was not as nice as her grandmother's property. The brush was mostly brown, and there weren't as many cedar trees, mostly shaggy-bark. It was also rockier. Good hiking boots were something Dale made her order online. Her grandmother's worked, but he said she needed a new pair that was the perfect size. She had been using them, and they felt good on her feet.

They set off at a slow pace, watching for footprints.

"He covers his prints whenever possible. His family likely hunted. He won't be as careful out here, though."

It took three hours.

Willow called out from ten feet away.

"He came through here," she said.

Dale smiled. "Good job," he said with obvious appreciation. Now the hunt begins."

CHAPTER THIRTY-FIVE

FOOTPRINTED EVIL

THE TRACKS DISAPPEARED INTO a narrow canyon, flanked by sheer rock walls and a scattering of jagged stones underfoot. Retracing their steps, they searched in vain, unable to pick up the trail again. By late morning, their growling stomachs made them pause to eat.

"Yum, my favorite," Willow said as Dale took the sandwiches from the backpack and handed her one.

"Your face says that's a lie, and you made the damn things," he accused good-naturedly.

"It was the only lunch we had in prison. Breakfast and dinner weren't much better, but at least it wasn't sandwiches." She noticed him shake his head. "I couldn't think of anything else to bring. Could you do better?"

He chuckled. "I would have made peanut butter and jelly instead of turkey."

"Ugh, that's worse."

"I'm a simple man," he teased.

Willow had packed chips and two cookies apiece. They ate in silence, watching the surrounding landscape. Crows flew overhead, reminding Willow of something Dale had said the first time she commented on them.

"Ravens are protected out here, and there's a heavy fine for harming one. The way to tell the difference between a raven and a crow is simple. If it's sitting on a fence, it's a raven. If it's flying overhead, it's a crow."

Dale loved to share these tidbits about living in the high desert. He was a good teacher, though sometimes, like with the crows, she didn't know if he was teasing or not. She had no intention of shooting ravens or crows, so she didn't dig deeper.

The ranch held a beauty Willow was only beginning to truly appreciate. With each step she explored, her connection to the land deepened, and she found herself falling in love with it more and more. She began to understand the reverence her grandmother had for this place and cherished the stories passed down about its history. Yet, beneath its breathtaking allure lay an unforgiving harshness and a deadly beauty Willow was learning to respect.

Their lunch break ended, and they started tracking again. Two hours later, Dale called it off.

"Don't look so disappointed," he said. "I promised Louisa we'd be back before dark, and we have several hours of hiking before we reach the truck. I don't want that woman on my bad side. We'll drive a bit farther tomorrow and start again. He's out here, and we'll find him."

Willow had no trouble falling asleep after the day of hiking and her lack of rest the previous night. She had also stopped worrying that Dale would kill Lance. If it happened, it would be in self-defense, and she would worry about the ramifications then.

They woke up at four, drank their coffee with a small breakfast, and started out again. Max and Daisy dutifully went to Louisa and Roger's. Willow didn't think Daisy's eyes could look sadder than they had when her foot was caught in the trap, but she proved her wrong.

"We'll be back," Willow assured her. Both Max and Daisy whined like the big babies they were.

After a quick hug from Louisa, they set out again. This time, Dale found the tracks. He called Willow over to show her the long trail of prints. They followed slowly, with Dale stopping to look around every fifty feet or so.

"I don't like it here," he said. "We're sitting ducks if he has a gun. We need to get out of this area quickly."

Dale had a rough map of the ranch folded in his pocket. It had property boundaries for each homestead.

"Too many people think they can handle the rough conditions out here," he told her as they walked. "They have no idea what it takes to haul water from town, the vehicle needed to do it, and the problems that come with having no electricity. It took me six months to save enough for a well, and that included using the last of my savings." He stopped and looked around before continuing, "Your place has a good solar system, but they're expensive. As you've learned, you still need to monitor electricity closely and do without things you wouldn't think twice about when you live on the grid."

"My grandmother said the well and solar were part of the property's price when she bought it."

"Yeah, she got lucky. If the property had been available before I bought mine, I would have snatched it up." They spoke in low tones while Dale kept constant vigilance.

The tracks ended after they crossed a deep ravine. They faced a steep series of large boulders, piled naturally over time, that rose more than thirty feet from the ground.

"We could go around," Dale said, "but I think we can make it to the top if you're game. We'll be able to see things better from up there. The ranch ends about twenty-five miles from here, and there are no more occupied properties out this far, the last time I checked."

Willow nodded, and they began their climb. Along the way, they encountered crevices deep enough to form small caves, which Dale carefully inspected for any signs of use. Finding nothing, they pressed on, though the ascent was far from straightforward. Several times, they had to backtrack when the rock ledges proved too steep to scale. Finally, after a challenging climb, they reached the summit.

In the wide expanse below, a solitary shack sat in an open field. A narrow, non-maintained dirt road led straight up to the front door. There was no vehicle or sign of life.

"That isn't marked on the map. It was most likely built by a squatter," Dale said quietly.

"Do you think he's in there?" Willow whispered.

"He may not be in there now, but I'd bet my boots this is the place he calls home," Dale assured her.

They found a spot between two boulders that partially hid them and offered a bit of shade. Dale tried to text Roger, but they were out of range.

"I need a favor," he said after two hours and no sign of movement below.

Willow nodded.

"If we stay here longer, Roger needs a text to know we may not make it back before dark. I need you to backtrack and send a text, so they don't worry about us. Can you do that?"

Willow didn't like it. They were safer together. Dale didn't let his steely eyes drop from hers. This was one of those times he would be stubborn.

"All right," she finally agreed. "I can run faster than an old man, so it's best I do it."

"I won't argue with you because it's true, even if you said it to get a rise out of me."

She stuck out her tongue, and he grinned.

Willow made it down the boulders, through the ravine, and another mile before the text would send. She didn't wait for a reply because she didn't want Dale up there alone. After hiking the ravine, she climbed about three feet. There was a deep crevasse to the side. It was the first Dale had checked, so she didn't bother looking. Her body was suddenly shoved from the side, and she lost her footing, falling hard onto the solid ground below and hitting her head. The world spun.

"Hi, bitch," the man said, his smile revealing a missing front tooth, making it more ominous. "Fancy meeting you here." He stood over her, blocking the sunlight. Her bleary mind told her this was Lance Hogg. He removed her gun from her holster before she had a chance to register what he was doing.

Dale would hear him. She had to trust Dale knew what he was doing. It would be okay. The words ran through her head as fear set in.

Lance stuck the gun in the back of his pants and pulled a large knife from the front. He leaned over, the knife coming down.

CHAPTER THIRTY-SIX

LESSONS FROM PRISON

S HE SHIED AWAY AND Lance stopped the blade inches from her face. "You think he's going to save you, but I already took care of that problem."

Her eyes remained fixed on the knife as he spoke, its menacing presence holding her attention. He had positioned it in front of her deliberately, and the grim realization finally hit her: streaks of blood stained the blade.

Her mind screamed, *No,* even as reality set in. He'd killed or seriously harmed Dale.

It was difficult not to curl in on herself and stop fighting. This thought was torn from her when Lance gripped her hair and dragged her several painful feet.

"You either walk, or I pull you by the hair," he said.

Another harsh tug had her struggling to stand upright. He headed away from the boulders and the area where they had hiked in. Had he been staying in a different section of the rock caves? He turned slightly, and she saw he wore Dale's backpack.

What little hope she had vanished.

Lance held the knife to his side unless she slowed. He used it to jab at the small of her back, where her shirt did little to cushion the sharp poke. He didn't cut her, but the threat was there. Her time in prison had given her the strength not to cry. She didn't want him to see her terror, or he would use it against her.

About a hundred feet from where she and Dale had climbed, a narrow canyon sliced through the boulders. The steep walls closed in tightly, leaving her barely enough space to move without brushing against the rough stone. Her mind raced, desperately searching for a way to escape or for something she could use as a weapon before he had a chance to reach for the gun. But there was nothing. As they moved closer to the gap in the boulders, he kept the knife's point pressed firmly against her back, ensuring she had no chance to escape.

"If you run, I'll shoot you," he said when they stepped into the field not far from the shack.

Willow walked dutifully forward.

"Open the door," Lance said.

She pushed the lever, and he gave her a hard shove inside. She fell to one knee, making it hard to turn, but she did.

The inside of the shack was a grim portrait of desperation and neglect. The dirt floor was uneven and scattered with trash: empty cans, small bones, and discarded clothing stained with grime. The walls, constructed from warped wooden planks, were streaked with dirt and splattered with unidentifiable stains. Sunlight filtered through the cracks, casting jagged lines of light across the squalor.

A rusted, iron cooking pot sat in one corner, next to a pile of stolen canned goods with faded labels. A plastic jug of water, only half full, rested against the wall.

The air was stale, carrying the acrid smell of sweat, old food, and something faintly metallic. A pile of ratty blankets lay balled up in another corner, serving as a crude bed.

The shack's single window was covered with a piece of torn fabric nailed unevenly into place. In the oppressive silence, the room felt suffocating. Lance had been living on the fringes of survival.

What he didn't know was that she had lived on a similar fringe.

"You look better in person than you do from far away," he leered.

Whether in prison or freedom, women knew *the look*. She'd seen the same look in her father's eyes, and she recognized it instantly. Her head pounded, and the walls seemed to slide sideways.

"Lay down before you fall," Lance said. "Your head is bleeding, and we'll take care of it before we have a little fun. I don't want you dying too quickly."

She was nauseous, terrified, and defiant all at once. If the end result was death, she would put up a fight and ruin what he thought would be a good time. She went to her knees beside the smelly blankets, then to her side, curling up to face him.

She blinked slowly. His fingers came near her face, and she jerked back. He pulled her hair again.

"Hold still while I check your damned eyes."

She froze and allowed him to peel back her eyelids. Only a little light came through the boards. She had no idea what he thought he was doing.

"I have water for your head wound. I'm going to lay the knife down behind me, but if you go for it or give me shit, I have no problem shooting you." He turned and placed the knife on the floor near the door.

She recognized the grip of Dale's gun in the back of his pants along with hers. If Dale was still alive, she could only save him by getting past Lance Hogg.

He lifted an empty can and poured water into it. It didn't look clean. Using a soiled shirt, he dampened it and wiped the blood from her wound. It was about an inch behind her ear.

She winced a bit more than was necessary, thinking that if he believed her weak, she might have a better chance of escape.

She also changed her mind about tears. Slowly, she allowed several to track down her cheeks. Her hands weren't trembling, so she reminded herself to add that to her act.

Lance finished cleaning the cut and rubbed one finger along her cheek. He licked the tear off and smiled at the taste.

"You're the old woman's granddaughter, aren't you?"

Did he know her story? She didn't see how he could. Her grandmother would never have told any of the Hoggs, including Carrie.

He backhanded her when she didn't answer. "The way this goes," he said, his voice shaking with anger, "is I ask questions, and you give me answers. If you don't, that pretty face will be bruised before I put it to good use. I don't want that, do you?"

"No," she said quickly, allowing her voice to quiver. She had nothing to lose, and she'd been in this situation before with her father. She was no longer twelve. She would fight Lance to the death. He would find little enjoyment in what he had planned.

"Now that's better," he murmured. "Was the old lady your grandmother?"

"She was. Her name was Joan."

He backhanded her again. "Smartass bitch, aren't you?"

It was better than being a dumbass, she thought silently. She pictured her mother's weakness and the years of abuse she suffered without fighting back. Her mother could have escaped, but she hadn't. Willow was more the product of her grandmother; of that, she had no doubt. She didn't have a plan, only years of built-up rage coursing through her veins. Rage that ran with Joan's blood.

"You lay there and don't move," he said, backing up.

He pulled off the backpack and unzipped the largest compartment. He began pulling out items. There were two packages of peanut butter crackers. He opened one and began shoving them into his mouth. Willow could see how thin he was. His weakness gave her hope.

He pulled out a flashlight and clicked it on, then off. Last, he pulled out a length of rope.

"Look what we have here," he said, his smile so wide she saw another missing tooth. "This will be fun," he added.

He was an idiot. Did he not remember the duct tape?

His eyes flashed to the other package of crackers.

"I'm hungry," she said softly.

"Shut up," he snapped. "If you're good, I'll let you have half."

She started crying, proud of her acting skills. "Don't hurt me, please."

He walked closer and squatted beside her, his hand reaching out to carefully take a few strands of hair between his fingers.

"I don't need to hurt you if you behave. I may even keep you around when I move into your place."

Her entire body shook with rage, but he wouldn't know that.

"Don't be afraid," he murmured. "You might like it."

He reached for his pants, unsnapped them, and began working on the zipper. He pushed them down his legs but didn't have a chance to finish.

Willow grabbed his ankles and rolled backward. His arms flailed, and he hit the dirt floor with a loud thud. His legs were trapped by his pants, and he hadn't remembered the guns, which tumbled out and hit the floor behind him. His eyes narrowed on the weapons, and she knew he would reach them first.

Fisting her hands, she brought them down with all the force she could muster, straight into his stomach. Foul air rushed from his mouth, and he curled inward. Willow kicked out, her foot connecting with his head. She practically dove over his body, but he struck out with his knee, catching her on the shoulder. She slammed against the wall.

Somehow, he leapt onto her, his fist raised above her face, ready to strike.

The door slammed open, and Dale rammed into Lance, knocking him away from her. She had no time to feel relieved; she dove for the guns.

Willow's heart thundered in her chest, the taste of blood sharp in her mouth. She blocked out the sounds of the fight and grasped the cold metal of the gun. Her body screamed in protest as she raised it, her mind flashing back to her father.

"Willow," Dale rasped as her vision cleared. "It's me."

Lance lay on the floor, Dale's boot pressing into his skull, forcing his head into the dirt.

Her hand dropped to her side.

"Grab the rope," he told her.

She grabbed the duct tape instead.

"This is a good start. I'll tie him up with both," Dale said. He proceeded to do exactly that.

"You're bleeding," Willow said, as the darkness cleared completely from her vision.

"I am, and I don't feel so good. Do you have your phone?" he asked.

She'd forgotten her cell and quickly grabbed it from her pocket.

"Check for a signal."

She shook her head.

"That's okay. How badly are you hurt?"

"I'm better than you, and not bleeding out in the dirt."

He chuckled softly, then dropped to his knees, his eyes going out of focus. Willow grabbed another filthy shirt and pressed it against his wound.

"I can hold it," he said. "You need to go for help."

Willow ran.

CHAPTER THIRTY-SEVEN

THE ONLY PLAN

Six weeks later...

"Just because the doctor gave you permission to move around some, doesn't mean, you kill yourself," Willow scolded.

"I'm old, but I'm not dead," Dale complained.

She smiled and gave him her sad face.

"Stop that," he grumbled, his hand coming up and swatting at her because she'd moved closer and tried to take the screwdriver away.

"You're the one who will stop. If you want something to do, tackle the dishes. You are not taking that screwdriver up the latter." Her hands were fisted on her hips, ready to do battle.

Dale handed the screwdriver to her and marched over to the couch and threw himself into it.

Willow knew his tantrums well. He was trying to install a security system that he'd ordered online. The doctor's orders of light exercise went right over his head. He'd been stabbed twice, once in the shoulder, and another more serious chest wound. Willow had no idea how he made it to the shack, and neither had the doctor who treated him.

Willow had only superficial scrapes and bruises that she barely felt. Dale had stayed in the hospital for a week. They'd both been interviewed. Willow told the truth, though she left out the details of her carrying a gun. Roger and Louisa had arrived first, and she'd left her holster in their truck before taking them to Dale.

He was unconscious by that time but breathing. The ride to the hospital had been harrowing because Willow just knew he would die.

Death was not in Dale Berger's mind, and he was too ornery to let Lance Hogg win. He was now too ornery about everything, but Willow wanted to talk to him. She'd been preparing this speech since he'd come home.

She took the chair and leaned forward, her hand reaching out to rub Max's back. Daisy jumped on the couch and lay beside Dale. He'd stopped shooing her off, because it was another fight against a female that he couldn't win.

"I've been thinking," she said.

"Very dangerous territory," he teased, his grumpiness gone.

"You told me to think about college, and I have. It's a no."

He raised his eyebrows but remained quiet.

My grandmother left me some money. It's not a whole bunch, but it's enough to start on a plan I can't get out of my mind." She looked at him, hoping he would see how serious she was and not make a joke about what she wanted to do.

"If you don't get to the point, I'll die of old age." His voice held laughter.

"You're not using your trailer." She stopped then continued before he said the obvious. "I want to help women like my mother and girls like me. What if we gave them a place to come and heal? A place to learn to defend themselves and also learn what they're capable of."

He stared at her for a long time. She couldn't tell what he was thinking. He finally shook his head, and grinned so wide, his jaw might lock in place.

"My property is worth some money," he said. "I don't need it. There are also places online, where you can raise money for good causes. I don't know anything about that crap, but you're smart and you can figure it out."

Willow launched herself from the chair and wrapped her arms around him, pushing him back against the couch.

"I don't need a ladder and screwdriver to kill me with you around." He was back to grumbling.

"I love you," she said.

"You sure do know how to get a man right in the heart," he said back.

Three months later

Dale hammered the last of nails into the ten-foot wooden posts that held the wrought-iron sign above the entrance to the driveway.

Dale had the iron twisted into a fancy script by one of the locals as a gift for Willow. She stepped back as Dale came off the ladder and joined her. They looked up at the entrance to Willow's property.

JOAN'S LEGACY

"I love it," Willow said.

"Joan would have loved it too."

EPILOGUE

UNSTOPPABLE, FIFTY MILES AWAY

THE LAND WAS QUIET as the sun dipped below the horizon, casting long shadows across the barren terrain. A lone coyote trotted through the scrub, its lean body moving with purpose. Its sharp ears twitched at the slightest rustle, its nose catching the faintest trace of scent on the dry wind.

In the distance, a Rabbit darted from the shelter of a bush, its movements jerky and frantic. The coyote froze, its golden eyes narrowing as it watched. Something about the prey was off. It moved erratically, its limbs stiff, its head twitching unnaturally. But hunger gnawed at the coyote's belly, and instinct overpowered caution.

The rabbit paused, its chest heaving as it turned its head to look back. Foam flecked its lips, and its wide eyes glistened with a feverish sheen. The coyote crept closer—its paws silent against the cracked earth. With a sudden burst of speed, the rabbit bolted, skittering through the scrub.

The chase was swift and brutal. The coyote surged forward, closing the distance with every stride. The Rabbit's speed faltered as its limbs betrayed it, trembling under the weight of its disease. With a final leap, the coyote pounced, its jaws closing around the small body. A brief struggle, a squeal of pain. And silence.

The coyote stood over its prey, panting. It began to tear into the flesh, unaware of the foam-streaked mouth or the tainted blood that stained its muzzle. The land seemed to hold its breath, the shadows deepening as the first stars pierced the twilight sky.

I am Rabies.

I am unstoppable.

About Holly

Holly S Roberts is an award-winning author which includes appearing on the USA TODAY list multiple times and selling more than one million books worldwide. Her career as a homicide and sex crimes detective kept her in the romance genre for a decade because she needed happy endings. After years of therapy and speaking publicly on matters close to her heart, she turned her pen to dark survival thrillers with kickass women that encapsulate her unique perspective. The Carter Family Shark Thrillers are current bestsellers. Holly's Detective Eve Bennet series is published by Hachette Books and her other titles are published independently. Max, her Rottweiler, is never far from her side because he listens when she has plot problems and offers rare insights when encouraged with cookies.